PENGUIN …

A Dissertation … and Other Essays

CHARLES LAMB (1775–1834) was an English essayist best known for his humorous *Essays of Elia*, from which the essay 'A Dissertation Upon Roast Pig' is taken. Lamb enjoyed a rich social life and became part of a group of young writers that included William Hazlitt, Percy Bysshe Shelley, Lord Byron and Samuel Taylor Coleridge, with whom he shared a lifelong friendship. Lamb never achieved the same literary success as his friends, but his influence on the English essay form cannot be overestimated, and his book *Specimens of the English Dramatic Poets* is remembered for popularizing the work of Shakespeare's contemporaries.

A Dissertation Upon Roast Pig and Other Essays

CHARLES LAMB

PENGUIN BOOKS

PENGUIN BOOKS

Published by the Penguin Group
Penguin Books Ltd, 80 Strand, London WC2R 0RL, England
Penguin Group (USA) Inc., 375 Hudson Street, New York, New York 10014, USA
Penguin Group (Canada), 90 Eglinton Avenue East, Suite 700, Toronto, Ontario, Canada M4P 2Y3 (a division of Pearson Penguin Canada Inc.)
Penguin Ireland, 25 St Stephen's Green, Dublin 2, Ireland (a division of Penguin Books Ltd)
Penguin Group (Australia), 250 Camberwell Road, Camberwell, Victoria 3124, Australia (a division of Pearson Australia Group Pty Ltd)
Penguin Books India Pvt Ltd, 11 Community Centre, Panchsheel Park, New Delhi – 110 017, India
Penguin Group (NZ), 67 Apollo Drive, Rosedale, Auckland 0632, New Zealand (a division of Pearson New Zealand Ltd)
Penguin Books (South Africa) (Pty) Ltd, 24 Sturdee Avenue, Rosebank, Johannesburg 2196, South Africa

Penguin Books Ltd, Registered Offices: 80 Strand, London WC2R 0RL, England

www.penguin.com

This collection published in Penguin Books 2011
This edition published for The Book People Ltd, 2011
Hall Wood Avenue, Haydock, St Helens, WA11 9UL
1

Set in 10.75/13pt Berkeley Oldstyle Book
Typeset by Jouve (UK), Milton Keynes
Printed in Great Britain by Clays Ltd, St Ives plc

Cover design based on a pattern for a saucer from the Derbyshire Porcelain original cup pattern books, no. 167, *c.* 1780–1810. (Photograph copyright © 2007 Derby Museums & Art Gallery.) Picture research by Samantha Johnson. Lettering by Stephen Raw

ISBN 978–0–241–96073–8

www.greenpenguin.co.uk

Contents

A Dissertation Upon Roast Pig

Mankind, says a Chinese manuscript, which my friend M. was obliging enough to read and explain to me, for the first seventy thousand ages ate their meat raw, clawing or biting it from the living animal, just as they do in Abyssinia to this day. This period is not obscurely hinted at by their great Confucius in the second chapter of his Mundane Mutations, where he designates a kind of golden age by the term Cho-fang, literally the Cooks' Holiday. The manuscript goes on to say, that the art of roasting, or rather broiling (which I take to be the elder brother) was accidentally discovered in the manner following. The swine-herd, Ho-ti, having gone out into the woods one morning, as his manner was, to collect mast for his hogs, left his cottage in the care of his eldest son Bo-bo, a great lubberly boy, who being fond of playing with fire, as younkers of his age commonly are, let some sparks escape into a bundle of straw, which kindling quickly, spread the conflagration over every part of their poor mansion, till it was reduced to ashes. Together with the cottage (a sorry antediluvian make-shift of a building, you may think it), what was of much more importance, a fine litter of new-farrowed pigs, no less than nine in number, perished. China pigs have been esteemed a luxury all over the East, from the remotest periods that we read of. Bo-bo was in the utmost consternation, as you may think, not so much for the sake of the tenement, which his father and he could easily build up again with a few dry branches, and the labour of an hour or two, at any time, as for the loss of the pigs.

While he was thinking what he should say to his father, and wringing his hands over the smoking remnants of one of those untimely sufferers, an odour assailed his nostrils, unlike any scent which he had before experienced. What could it proceed from? – not from the burnt cottage – he had smelt that smell before – indeed this was by no means the first accident of the kind which had occurred through the negligence of this unlucky young fire-brand. Much less did it resemble that of any known herb, weed, or flower. A premonitory moistening at the same time overflowed his nether lip. He knew not what to think. He next stooped down to feel the pig, if there were any signs of life in it. He burnt his fingers, and to cool them he applied them in his booby fashion to his mouth. Some of the crumbs of the scorched skin had come away with his fingers, and for the first time in his life (in the world's life indeed, for before him no man had known it) he tasted – *crackling!* Again he felt and fumbled at the pig. It did not burn him so much now, still he licked his fingers from a sort of habit. The truth at length broke into his slow understanding, that it was the pig that smelt so, and the pig that tasted so delicious; and surrendering himself up to the new-born pleasure, be fell to tearing up whole handfuls of the scorched skin with the flesh next it, and was cramming it down his throat in his beastly fashion, when his sire entered amid the smoking rafters, armed with retributory cudgel, and finding how affairs stood, began to rain blows upon the young rogue's shoulders, as thick as hail-stones, which Bo-bo heeded not any more than if they had been flies. The tickling pleasure, which he experienced in his lower regions, had rendered him quite callous to any inconveniences be might feel in those remote quarters. His father might lay on, but he could not beat him from his pig, till he had fairly made an end of it, when, becoming a little more sensible of his situation, something like the following dialogue ensued.

'You graceless whelp, what have you got there devouring? Is it not enough that you have burnt me down three houses with your dog's tricks, and be hanged to you! but you must be eating fire, and I know not what – what have you got there, I say?'

'O, father, the pig, the pig! do come and taste how nice the burnt pig eats.'

The ears of Ho-ti tingled with horror. He cursed his son, and he cursed himself that ever he should beget a son that should eat burnt pig.

Bo-bo, whose scent was wonderfully sharpened since morning, soon raked out another pig, and fairly rending it asunder, thrust the lesser half by main force into the fists of Ho-ti, still shouting out, 'Eat, eat, eat the burnt pig, father, only taste – O Lord!' – with such-like barbarous ejaculations, cramming all the while as if he would choke.

Ho-ti trembled every joint while he grasped the abominable thing, wavering whether he should not put his son to death for an unnatural young monster, when the crackling scorching his fingers, as it had done his son's, and applying the same remedy to them, he in his turn tasted some of its flavour, which, make what sour mouths he would for a pretence, proved not altogether displeasing to him. In conclusion (for the manuscript here is a little tedious), both father and son fairly sat down to the mess, and never left off till they had despatched all that remained of the litter.

Bo-bo was strictly enjoined not to let the secret escape, for the neighbours would certainly have stoned them for a couple of abominable wretches, who could think of improving upon the good meat which God had sent them. Nevertheless, strange stories got about. It was observed that Ho-ti's cottage was burnt down now more frequently than ever. Nothing but fires from this time forward. Some would break out in broad day, others in the night-time. As often as the sow farrowed, so sure was the house of Ho-ti to be in a blaze; and Ho-ti himself, which was the more remarkable, instead of chastising his son, seemed to grow more indulgent to him than ever. At length they were watched, the terrible mystery discovered, and father and son summoned to take their trial at Pekin, then an inconsiderable assize town. Evidence was given, the obnoxious food itself produced in court, and verdict about to be pronounced, when the foreman of the jury begged that some of the burnt pig, of which the culprits stood accused, might be handed into the box. He handled it, and they all handled it; and burning their fingers, as Bo-bo and his father had done before them, and nature prompting to each of them the same remedy, against the face of all the facts, and the clearest charge which judge had ever given, – to the surprise of the whole court, townsfolk, strangers, reporters, and all present – without leaving the box, or any manner of consultation whatever, they brought in a simultaneous verdict of Not Guilty.

The judge, who was a shrewd fellow, winked at the manifest iniquity of the decision: and when the court was dismissed, went privily and bought up all the pigs that could be had for love or money. In a few days his lordship's town-house was observed to be on fire. The thing took wing, and now there was nothing to be seen but fire in every direction. Fuel and pigs grew enormously dear all over the district. The insurance-offices one and all shut up shop. People built slighter and slighter every day, until it was feared that the very science of architecture would in no long time be lost to the world. Thus this custom of firing houses continued, till in process of time, says my manuscript, a sage arose, like our Locke, who made a discovery that the flesh of swine, or indeed of any other animal, might be cooked (*burnt*, as they called it) without the necessity of consuming a whole house to dress it. Then first began the rude form of a gridiron. Roasting by the string or spit came in a century or two later, I forget in whose dynasty. By such slow degrees, concludes the manuscript, do the most useful, and seemingly the most obvious, arts make their way among mankind —

Without placing too implicit faith in the account above given, it must be agreed that if a worthy pretext for so dangerous an experiment as setting houses on fire (especially in these days) could be assigned in favour of any culinary object, that pretext and excuse might be found in ROAST PIG.

Of all the delicacies in the whole *mundus edibiles*, I will maintain it to be the most delicate – *princeps obsoniorum*.

I speak not of your grown porkers – things between pig and pork – those hobbydehoys – but a young and tender suckling – under a moon old – guiltless as yet of the sty – with no original speck of the *amor immunditiæ*, the hereditary failing of the first parent, yet manifest – his voice as yet not broken, but something between a childish treble and a grumble – the mild forerunner or *præludium* of a grunt.

He must be roasted. I am not ignorant that our ancestors ate them seethed, or boiled – but what a sacrifice of the exterior tegument!

There is no flavour comparable, I will contend, to that of the crisp, tawny, well-watched, not over-roasted, *crackling*, as it is well called – the very teeth are invited to their share of the pleasure at this banquet in overcoming the coy, brittle resistance – with the adhesive oleaginous – O call it not fat! but an indefinable sweetness growing up to it – the tender blossoming of fat – fat cropped in the bud – taken in the shoot – in the first innocence – the cream and quintessence of the child-pig's yet pure food — the lean, no lean, but a kind of animal manna – or, rather, fat and lean (if it must be so) so blended and running into each other, that both together make but one ambrosian result or common substance.

Behold him, while he is 'doing' – it seemeth rather a

refreshing warmth, than a scorching heat, that he is so passive to. How equably he twirleth round the string! – Now he is just done. To see the extreme sensibility of that tender age! he hath wept out his pretty eyes – radiant jellies – shooting stars. –

See him in the dish, his second cradle, how meek he lieth! – wouldst thou have had this innocent grow up to the grossness and indocility which too often accompany maturer swinehood? Ten to one he would have proved a glutton, a sloven, an obstinate, disagreeable animal – wallowing in all manner of filthy conversation – from these sins he is happily snatched away –

> Ere sin could blight or sorrow fade,
> Death came with timely care –

his memory is odoriferous – no clown curseth, while his stomach half rejecteth, the rank bacon – no coalheaver bolteth him in reeking sausages – he hath a fair sepulchre in the grateful stomach of the judicious epicure – and for such a tomb might be content to die.

He is the best of sapors. Pine-apple is great. She is indeed almost too trancendent – a delight, if not sinful, yet so like to sinning that really a tender-conscienced person would do well to pause – too ravishing for mortal taste, she woundeth and excoriateth the lips that approach her – like lovers' kisses, she biteth – she is a pleasure bordering on pain from the fierceness and insanity of her relish – but she stoppeth at the palate – she meddleth not with the appetite – and the coarsest hunger might barter her consistently for a mutton-chop.

Pig – let me speak his praise – is no less provocative of the appetite, than he is satisfactory to the criticalness of the censorious palate. The strong man may batten on him, and the weakling refuseth not his mild juices.

Unlike to mankind's mixed characters, a bundle of virtues and vices, inexplicably intertwisted, and not to be unravelled without hazard, he is – good throughout. No part of him is better or worse than another. He helpeth, as far as his little means extend, all around. He is the least envious of banquets. He is all neighbours' fare.

I am one of those, who freely and ungrudgingly impart a share of the good things of this life which fall to their lot (few as mine are in this kind) to a friend. I protest I take as great an interest in my friend's pleasures, his relishes, and proper satisfactions, as in mine own. 'Presents,' I often say, 'endear Absents.' Hares, pheasants, partridges, snipes, barn-door chickens (those 'tame villatic fowl,') capons, plovers, brawn, barrels of oysters, I dispense as freely as I receive them. I love to taste them, as it were, upon the tongue of my friend. But a stop must be put somewhere. One would not, like Lear, 'give everything.' I make my stand upon pig. Methinks it is an ingratitude to the Giver of all good flavours to extra-domiciliate, or send out of the house slightingly (under pretext of friendship, or I know not what) a blessing so particularly adapted, predestined, I may say, to my individual palate. – It argues an insensibility.

I remember a touch of conscience in this kind at school. My good old aunt, who never parted from me at the end of a holiday without stuffing a sweetmeat, or some nice thing into my pocket, had dismissed me one evening with a smoking plum-cake, fresh from the oven. In my way to school (it was over London bridge) a grey-headed old beggar saluted me (I have no doubt, at this time of day that he was a counterfeit.) I had no pence to console him with, and in the vanity of self-denial, and the very coxcombry of charity, schoolboy-like, I made him a present of – the whole cake! I walked on a little, buoyed up, as one is on such occasions, with a sweet soothing of self-satisfaction; but before I had got to the end of the bridge, my better feelings returned, and I burst into tears, thinking how ungrateful I had been to my good aunt, to go and give her good gift away to a stranger that I had never seen before, and who might be a bad man for aught I knew; and then I thought of the pleasure my aunt would be taking in thinking that I – I myself, and not another – would eat her nice cake – and what should I say to her the next time I saw her – how naughty I was to part with her pretty present! – and the odour of that spicy cake came back upon my recollection, and the pleasure and the curiosity I had taken in seeing her make it, and her joy when she sent it to the oven, and how disappointed she would feel that I had never had a bit of it in my mouth at last – and I blamed my impertinent spirit of almsgiving, and out-of-place hypocrisy of goodness; and above all I wished never to see the face again of that insidious, good-for-nothing, old grey impostor.

Our ancestors were nice in their method of sacrificing these tender victims. We read of pigs whipt to death with something of a shock, as we hear of any other obsolete custom. The age of discipline is gone by, or it would be curious to inquire (in a philosophical light merely) what effect this process might have towards intenerating and dulcifying a substance, naturally so mild and dulcet as the flesh of young pigs. It looks like refining a violet. Yet we should be cautious, while we condemn the inhumanity, how we censure the wisdom of the practice. It might impart a gusto. –

I remember an hypothesis, argued upon by the young students, when I was at St. Omer's, and maintained with much learning and pleasantry on both sides, 'Whether, supposing that the flavour of a pig who obtained his death by whipping (*per flagellationem extremam*) superadded a pleasure upon the palate of a man more intense than any possible suffering we can conceive in the animal, is man justified in using that method of putting the animal to death?' I forget the decision.

His sauce should be considered. Decidedly, a few bread crumbs, done up with his liver and brains, and a dash of mild sage. But banish, dear Mrs. Cook, I beseech you, the whole onion tribe. Barbecue your whole hogs to your palate, steep them in shalots, stuff them out with plantations of the rank and guilty garlic; you cannot poison them, or make them stronger than they are – but consider, he is a weakling – a flower.

Grace Before Meat

The custom of saying grace at meals had, probably, its origin in the early times of the world, and the hunter-state of man, when dinners were precarious things, and a full meal was something more than a common blessing! when a belly-full was a wind-fall, and looked like a special providence. In the shouts and triumphal songs with which, after a season of sharp abstinence, a lucky booty of deer's or goat's flesh would naturally be ushered home, existed, perhaps, the germ of the modern grace. It is not otherwise easy to be understood, why the blessing of food – the act of eating – should have had a particular expression of thanksgiving annexed to it, distinct from that implied and silent gratitude with which we are expected to enter upon the enjoyment of the many other various gifts and good things of existence.

I own that I am disposed to say grace upon twenty other occasions in the course of the day besides my dinner. I want a form for setting out upon a pleasant walk, for a moonlight ramble, for a friendly meeting, or a solved problem. Why have we none for books, those spiritual repasts – a grace before Milton – a grace before Shakspeare – a devotional exercise proper to be said before reading the Fairy Queen? – but the received ritual having prescribed these forms to the solitary ceremony of manducation, I shall confine my observations to the experience which I have had of the grace, properly so called; commending my new scheme for extension to a niche in the grand philosophical, poetical, and perchance in part heretical, liturgy, now compiling by my friend Homo Humanus, for the use of a certain snug congregation of Utopian Rabelæsian Christians, no matter where assembled.

The form, then, of the benediction before eating has its beauty at a poor man's table, or at the simple and unprovocative repast of children. It is here that the grace becomes exceedingly graceful. The indigent man, who hardly knows whether he shall have a meal the next day or not, sits down to his fare with a present sense of the blessing, which can be but feebly acted by the rich, into whose minds the conception of wanting a dinner could never, but by some extreme theory, have entered. The proper end of food – the animal sustenance – is barely contemplated by them. The poor man's bread is his daily bread, literally his bread for the day. Their courses are perennial.

Again the plainest diet seems the fittest to be preceded by the grace. That which is least stimulative to appetite, leaves the mind most free for foreign considerations. A man may feel thankful, heartily thankful, over a dish of plain mutton with turnips, and have leisure to reflect upon the ordinance and institution of eating; when he shall confess a perturbation of mind, inconsistent with the purposes of the grace, at the presence of venison or turtle. When I have sate (a *rarus hospes*) at rich men's tables, with the savoury soup and messes steaming up the nostrils, and moistening the lips of the guests with desire and a distracted choice, I have felt the introduction of that ceremony to be unseasonable. With the ravenous orgasm upon you, it seems impertinent to interpose a religious sentiment. It is a confusion of purpose to mutter out praises from a mouth that waters. The heats of epicurism put out the gentle flame of devotion. The incense which rises round is pagan, and the belly-god intercepts it for his own. The very excess of the provision beyond the needs, takes away all sense of proportion between the end and means. The giver is veiled by his gifts. You are startled at the injustice of returning thanks – for what? – for having too much, while so many starve. It is to praise the Gods amiss.

I have observed this awkwardness felt, scarce consciously perhaps, by the good man who says the grace. I have seen it in clergymen and others – a sort of shame – a sense of the co-presence of circumstances which unhallow the blessing. After a devotional tone put on for a few seconds, how rapidly the speaker will fall into his common voice! helping himself or his neighbour, as if to get rid of some uneasy sensation of hypocrisy. Not that the good man was a hypocrite, or was not most conscientious in the discharge of the duty; but he felt in his inmost mind the incompatibility of the scene and the viands before him with the exercise of a calm and rational gratitude.

I hear somebody exclaim, – Would you have Christians sit down at table, like hogs to their troughs, without remembering the Giver? – no – I would have them sit down as Christians, remembering the Giver, and less like hogs. Or if their appetites must run riot, and they must pamper themselves with delicacies for which east and west are ransacked, I would have them postpone their benediction to a fitter season, when appetite is laid; when the still small voice can be heard, and the reason of the grace returns – with temperate diet and restricted dishes. Gluttony and surfeiting are no proper occasions for thanksgiving. When Jeshurum waxed fat, we read that he kicked. Virgil knew the harpy-nature better, when he put into the mouth of Celæno anything but a blessing. We may be gratefully sensible of the deliciousness of some kinds of food beyond others, though that is a meaner and inferior gratitude: but the proper object of the grace is sustenance, not relishes; daily bread, not delicacies; the means of life, and not the means of pampering the carcass. With what frame or composure, I wonder, can a city chaplain pronounce his benediction at some great Hall-feast, when he knows that his last concluding pious word – and that in all probability, the sacred name which he preaches – is but the signal for so many impatient harpies to commence their foul orgies, with as little sense of true thankfulness (which is temperance) as those Virgilian fowl! It is well if the good man himself does not feel his devotions a little clouded, those foggy sensuous steams mingling with and polluting the pure altar sacrifice.

The severest satire upon full tables and surfeits is the banquet which Satan, in the 'Paradise Regained,' provides for a temptation in the wilderness:

> A table richly spread in regal mode
> With dishes piled, and meats of noblest sort

And savour; beasts of chase, or fowl of game,
In pastry built, or from the spit, or boiled,
Gris-amber-steamed; all fish from sea or shore,
Freshet or purling brook, for which was drained
Pontus, and Lucrine bay, and Afric coast.

The Tempter, I warrant you, thought these cates would go down without the recommendatory preface of a benediction. They are like to be short graces where the devil plays the host. – I am afraid the poet wants his usual decorum in this place. Was he thinking of the old Roman luxury, or of a gaudy day at Cambridge? This was a temptation fitter for a Heliogabalus. The whole banquet is too civic and culinary, and the accompaniments altogether a profanation of that deep, abstracted holy scene. The mighty artillery of sauces, which the cook-fiend conjures up, is out of proportion to the simple wants and plain hunger of the guest. He that disturbed him in his dreams, from his dreams might have been taught better. To the temperate fantasies of the famished Son of God, what sort of feasts presented themselves? – He dreamed indeed,

— As appetite is wont to dream,
Of meats and drinks, nature's refreshment sweet.

But what meats? –

Him thought, he by the brook of Cherith stood,
And saw the ravens with their horny beaks
Food to Elijah bringing even and morn;
Though ravenous, taught to abstain from what they
  brought;

He saw the prophet also how he fled
Into the desert and how there he slept
Under a juniper; then how awaked
He found his supper on the coals prepared,
And by the angel was bid rise and eat,
And ate the second time after repose,
The strength whereof sufficed him forty days:
Sometimes, that with Elijah he partook,
Or as a guest with Daniel at his pulse.

Nothing in Milton is finelier fancied than these temperate dreams of the divine Hungerer. To which of these two visionary banquets, think you, would the introduction of what is called the grace have been the most fitting and pertinent?

Theoretically I am no enemy to graces; but practically I own that (before meat especially) they seem to involve something awkward and unseasonable. Our appetites, of one or another kind, are excellent spurs to our reason, which might otherwise but feebly set about the great ends of preserving and continuing the species. They are fit blessings to be contemplated at a distance with a becoming gratitude; but the moment of appetite (the judicious reader will apprehend me) is, perhaps, the least fit season for that exercise. The Quakers, who go about their business of every description with more calmness than we, have more title to the use of these benedictory prefaces. I have always admired their silent grace, and the more because I have observed their applications to the meat and drink following to be less passionate and sensual than ours. They are neither gluttons nor wine-bibbers as a people. They eat, as a horse bolts his chopped hay, with indifference, calmness, and cleanly circumstances. They neither grease nor slop themselves. When I see a citizen in his bib and tucker, I cannot imagine it a surplice.

I am no Quaker at my food. I confess I am not indifferent to the kinds of it. Those unctuous morsels of deer's flesh were not made to be received with dispassionate services. I hate a man who swallows it, affecting not to know what he is eating. I suspect his taste in higher matters. I shrink instinctively from one who professes to like minced veal. There is a physiognomical character in the tastes for food. C—— holds that a man cannot have a pure mind who refuses apple-dumplings. I am not certain but he is right. With the decay of my first innocence, I confess a less and less relish daily for those innocuous cates. The whole vegetable tribe have lost their gust with me. Only I stick to asparagus, which still seems to inspire gentle thoughts. I am impatient and querulous under culinary disappointments, as to come home at the dinner hour, for instance, expecting some savoury mess, and to find one quite tasteless and sapidless. Butter ill melted – that commonest of kitchen failures – puts me beside my tenor. – The author of the Rambler used to make inarticulate animal noises over a favourite food. Was this the music quite proper to be preceded by the grace? or would the pious man have done better to postpone his devotions to a season when the blessing might be contemplated with less perturbation? I quarrel with no man's tastes, nor would set my thin face against those excellent things, in their way, jollity and feasting. But as these exercises, however laudable, have little in them of grace or gracefulness, a man should be sure, before he ventures so to grace them, that while he is pretending his devotions otherwhere, he is not secretly kissing his hand to some great fish – his Dagon – with a special consecration of no ark but the fat tureen before him. Graces are the sweet preluding strains to the banquets of angels and children; to the roots and severer repasts of the Chartreuse; to the slender, but not slenderly acknowledged, refection of the poor and humble man: but at the heaped-up boards of the pampered and the luxurious they become of dissonant mood, less timed and tuned to the occasion, methinks, than the noise of those better befitting organs would be which children hear tales of, at Hog's Norton. We sit too long at our meals, or are too curious in the study of them, or too disordered in our application to them, or engross too great a portion of those good things (which should be common) to our share, to be able with any grace to say grace. To be thankful for what we grasp exceeding our proportion, is to add hypocrisy to injustice. A lurking sense of this truth is what makes the performance of this duty so cold and spiritless a service at most tables. In houses where the grace is as indispensable as the napkin, who has not seen that never-settled question arise, as to *who shall say it?* while the good man of the house and the visitor clergyman, or some other guest belike of next authority, from years or gravity, shall be bandying about the office between them as a matter of compliment, each of them not unwilling to shift the awkward burthen of an equivocal duty from his own shoulders?

I once drank tea in company with two Methodist divines of different persuasions, whom it was my fortune to introduce to each other for the first time that evening. Before the first cup was handed round, one of these reverend gentlemen put it to the other, with all due solemnity, whether he chose to *say anything*. It seems it is the custom with some sectaries to put up a short prayer before this meal also. His reverend brother did not at first quite apprehend him, but upon an explanation, with little less importance he made answer that it was not a custom known in his church: in which courteous evasion the other acquiescing for good manners' sake, or in compliance with a weak brother, the supplementary or tea-grace was waived altogether. With what spirit might not Lucian have painted two priests, of *his* religion, playing into each other's hands the compliment of performing or omitting a sacrifice, – the hungry God meantime, doubtful of his incense, with expectant nostrils hovering over the two flamens, and (as between two stools) going away in the end without his supper.

A short form upon these occasions is felt to want reverence; a long one, I am afraid, cannot escape the charge of impertinence. I do not quite approve of the epigrammatic conciseness with which that equivocal wag (but my pleasant school-fellow) C. V. L., when importuned for a grace, used to inquire, first slyly leering down the table, 'Is there no clergyman here,' – significantly adding, 'Thank G –.' Nor do I think our old form at school quite pertinent, where we were used to preface our bald bread-and-cheese suppers with a preamble, connecting with that humble blessing a recognition of benefits the most awful and overwhelming to the imagination which religion has to offer. *Non tunc illis erat locus.* I remember we were put to it to reconcile the phrase 'good creatures,' upon which the blessing rested, with the fare set before us, wilfully understanding that expression in a low and animal sense, – till some one recalled a legend, which told how, in the golden days of Christ's, the young Hospitallers were wont to have smoking joints of roast meat upon their nightly boards, till some pious benefactor, commiserating the decencies, rather than the palates, of the children, commuted our flesh for garments, and gave us – *horresco referens* – trousers instead of mutton.

The Praise of Chimney-Sweepers

I like to meet a sweep – understand me – not a grown sweeper – old chimney-sweepers are by no means attractive – but one of those tender novices, blooming through their first nigritude, the maternal washings not quite effaced from the cheek – such as come forth with the dawn, or somewhat earlier, with their little professional notes sounding like the *peep peep* of a young sparrow; or liker to the matin lark should I pronounce them, in their aërial ascents not seldom anticipating the sun-rise?

I have a kindly yearning toward these dim specks – poor blots – innocent blacknesses –

I reverence these young Africans of our own growth – these almost clergy imps, who sport their cloth without assumption; and from their little pulpits (the tops of chimneys,) in the nipping air of a December morning, preach a lesson of patience to mankind.

When a child, what a mysterious pleasure it was to witness their operation! to see a chit no bigger than one's-self, enter, one knew not by what process, into what seemed the *fauces Averni* – to pursue him in imagination, as he went sounding on through so many dark stifling caverns, horrid shades! to shudder with the idea that 'now, surely, he must be lost forever!' – to revive at hearing his feeble shout of discovered day-light – and then (O fulness of delight!) running out of doors, to come just in time to see the sable phenomenon emerge in safety, the brandished weapon of his art victorious like some flag waved over a conquered citadel! I seem to remember having been told, that a bad sweep was once left in a stack with his brush, to indicate which way the wind blew. It was an awful spectacle certainly; not much unlike the old stage direction in Macbeth, where the 'Apparition of a child crowned, with a tree in his hand, rises.'

Reader, if thou meetest one of these small gentry in thy early rambles, it is good to give him a penny. It is better to give him twopence. If it be starving weather, and to the proper troubles of his hard occupation, a pair of kibed heels (no unusual accompaniment) be superadded, the demand on thy humanity will surely rise to a tester.

There is a composition, the ground-work of which I have understood to be the sweet wood 'yclept sassafras. This wood boiled down to a kind of tea, and tempered with an infusion of milk and sugar, hath to some tastes a delicacy beyond the China luxury. I know not how thy palate may relish it; for myself, with every deference to the judicious Mr. Read, who hath time out of mind kept open a shop (the only one he avers in London) for the vending of this 'wholesome and pleasant beverage,' on the south-side of Fleet-street, as thou approachest Bridge-street – *the only Salopian house* – I have never yet adventured to dip my own particular lip in a basin of his commended ingredients – a cautious premonition to the olfactories constantly whispering to me, that my stomach must infallibly, with all due courtesy, decline it. Yet I have seen palates, otherwise not uninstructed in dietetical elegancies, sup it up with avidity.

I know not by what particular conformation of the organ it happens, but I have always found that this composition is surprisingly gratifying to the palate of a young chimney-sweeper – whether the oily particles (sassafras is slightly oleaginous) do attenuate and soften the fuliginous concretions, which are sometimes found (in dissections) to adhere to the roof of the mouth in these unfledged practitioners; or whether Nature, sensible that she had mingled too much of bitter wood in the lot of these raw victims, caused to grow out of the earth her sassafras for a sweet lenitive – but so it is, that no possible taste or odour to the senses of a young chimney-sweeper can convey a delicate excitement comparable to this mixture. Being penniless, they will yet hang their black heads over the ascending steam, to gratify one sense if possible, seemingly no less pleased than those domestic animals – cats – when they purr over a new-found spring of valerian. There is something more in these sympathies than philosophy can inculcate.

Now albeit Mr. Read boasteth, not without reason, that his is the *only Salopian house;* yet be it known to thee, reader – if thou art one who keepest what are called good hours, thou art haply ignorant of the fact – he hath a race of industrious imitators, who from stalls, and under open sky, dispense the same savoury mess to humbler customers, at that dead time of the dawn, when (as extremes meet) the rake, reeling home from his midnight cups, and the hard-handed artisan leaving his bed to resume the premature labours of the day, jostle, not unfrequently to the manifest disconcerting of the former, for the honours of the pavement. It is the time when, in summer, between the expired and the not yet relumined kitchen-fires, the kennels of our fair metropolis give forth their least satisfactory odours. The rake, who wisheth to dissipate his o'ernight vapours in more grateful coffee, curses the ungenial fume, as he passeth; but the artisan stops to taste, and blesses the fragrant breakfast.

This is *saloop* – the precocious herb-woman's darling – the delight of the early gardener, who transports his smoking cabbages by break of day from Hammersmith to Covent-garden's famed piazzas – the delight, and oh! I fear, too often the envy, of the unpennied sweep. Him, shouldst thou haply encounter, with his dim visage pendent over the grateful steam, regale him with a sumptuous basin (it will cost but three-halfpennies) and a slice of delicate bread and butter (an added halfpenny) – so may thy culinary fires, eased of the o'er-charged secretions from thy worse-placed hospitalities, curl up a lighter volume to the welkin – so may the descending soot never taint thy costly well-ingredienced soups – nor the odious cry, quick-reaching from street to street, of the *fired chimney*, invite the rattling engines from ten adjacent parishes, to disturb for a casual scintillation thy peace and pocket!

I am by nature extremely susceptible of street affronts; the jeers and taunts of the populace; the low-bred triumph they display over the casual trip, or splashed stocking, of a gentleman. Yet can I endure the jocularity of a young sweep with something more than forgiveness. – In the last winter but one, pacing along Cheapside with my accustomed precipitation when I walk westward, a treacherous slide brought me upon my back in an instant. I scrambled up with pain and shame enough – yet outwardly trying to face it down, as if nothing had happened – when the roguish grin of one of these young wits encountered me. There he stood, pointing me out with his dusky finger to the mob, and to a poor woman (I suppose his mother) in particular, till the tears for the exquisiteness of the fun (so he thought it) worked themselves out at the corners of his poor red eyes, red from many a previous weeping, and soot-inflamed, yet twinkling through all with such a joy, snatched out of desolation, that Hogarth —— but Hogarth has got him already (how could he miss him?) in the March to Finchley, grinning at the pieman – there he stood, as he stands in the picture, irremovable, as if the jest was to last for ever – with such a maximum of glee, and minimum of mischief, in his mirth – for the grin of a genuine sweep hath absolutely no malice in it – that I could have been content, if the honour of a gentleman might endure it, to have remained his butt and his mockery till midnight.

I am by theory obdurate to the seductiveness of what are called a fine set of teeth. Every pair of rosy lips (the ladies must pardon me) is a casket presumably holding such jewels; but, methinks, they should take leave to 'air' them as frugally as possible. The fine lady, or fine gentleman, who show me their teeth, show me bones. Yet must I confess, that from the mouth of a true sweep a display (even to ostentation) of those white and shining ossifications, strikes me as an agreeable anomaly in manners, and an allowable piece of foppery. It is, as when

A sable cloud
Turns forth her silver lining on the night.

It is like some remnant of gentry not quite extinct; a badge of better days; a hint of nobility: – and, doubtless, under the obscuring darkness and double night of their forlorn disguisement, oftentimes lurketh good blood, and gentle conditions, derived from lost ancestry, and a lapsed pedigree. The premature apprenticements of these tender victims give but too much encouragement, I fear, to clandestine and almost infantile abductions; the seeds of civility and true courtesy, so often discernible in these young grafts (not otherwise to be accounted for) plainly hint at some forced adoptions; many noble Rachels mourning for their children, even in our days, countenance the fact; the tales of fairy-spiriting may shadow a lamentable verity, and the recovery of the young Montague be but a solitary instance of good fortune out of many irreparable and hopeless *defiliations*.

In one of the state-beds at Arundel Castle, a few years since – under a ducal canopy – (that seat of the Howards is an object of curiosity to visitors, chiefly for its beds, in which the late duke was especially a connoisseur) – encircled with curtains of delicatest crimson, with starry coronets inwoven – folded between a pair of sheets whiter and softer than the lap where Venus lulled Ascanius – was discovered by chance, after all methods of search had failed, at noon-day, fast asleep, a lost chimney-sweeper. The little creature, having somehow confounded his passage among the intricacies of those lordly chimneys, by some unknown aperture had alighted upon this magnificent chamber; and, tired with his tedious explorations, was unable to resist the delicious invitement to repose, which he there saw exhibited; so creeping between the sheets very quietly, laid his black head upon the pillow, and slept like a young Howard.

Such is the account given to the visiters at the Castle. – But I cannot help seeming to perceive a confirmation of what I had just hinted at in this story. A high instinct was at work in the case, or I am mistaken. Is it probable that a poor child of that description, with whatever weariness he might be visited, would have ventured, under such a penalty as he would be taught to expect, to uncover the sheets of a Duke's bed, and deliberately to lay himself down between them, when the rug, or the carpet, presented an obvious couch, still far above his pretensions – is this probable, I would ask, if the great power of nature, which I contend for, had not been manifested within him, prompting to the adventure? Doubtless this young nobleman (for such my mind misgives me that he must be) was allured by some memory, not amounting to full consciousness, of his condition in infancy, when he was used to be lapped by his mother, or his nurse, in just such sheets as he there found, into which he was now but creeping back as into his proper *incunabula*, and resting-place. – By no other theory than by this sentiment of a pre-existent state (as I may call it), can I explain a deed so venturous, and, indeed, upon any other system, so indecorous, in this tender, but unseasonable, sleeper.

My pleasant friend JEM WHITE was so impressed with a belief of metamorphoses like this frequently taking place, that in some sort to reverse the wrongs of fortune in these poor changelings, he instituted an annual feast of chimney-sweepers, at which it was his pleasure to officiate as host and waiter. It was a solemn supper held in Smithfield, upon the yearly return of the fair of St. Bartholomew. Cards were issued a week before to the master-sweeps in and about the metropolis, confining the invitation to their younger fry. Now and then an elderly stripling would get in among us, and be good-naturedly winked at; but our main body were infantry. One unfortunate wight indeed, who, relying upon his dusky suit, had intruded himself into our party, but by tokens was providentially discovered in time to be no chimney-sweeper, (all is not soot which looks so,) was quoited out of the presence with universal indignation, as not having on the wedding garment; but in general the greatest harmony prevailed. The place chosen was a convenient spot among the pens, at the north side of the fair, not so far distant as to be impervious to the agreeable hubbub of that vanity; but remote enough not to be obvious to the interruption of every gaping spectator in it. The guests assembled about seven. In those little temporary parlours three tables were spread with napery, not so fine as substantial, and at every board a comely hostess presided with her pan of hissing sausages. The nostrils of the young rogues dilated at the savour.

JAMES WHITE, as head waiter, had charge of the first table; and myself, with our trusty companion BIGOD, ordinarily ministered to the other two. There was clambering and jostling, you may be sure, who should get at the first table – for Rochester in his maddest days could not have done the humours of the scene with more spirit than my friend. After some general expression of thanks for the honour the company had done him, his inaugural ceremony was to clasp the greasy waist of old dame Ursula (the fattest of the three), that stood frying and fretting, half-blessing, half-cursing 'the gentleman,' and imprint upon her chaste lips a tender salute, whereat the universal host would set up a shout that tore the concave, while hundreds of grinning teeth startled the night with their brightness. O it was a pleasure to see the sable younkers lick in the unctuous meat, with *his* more unctuous sayings – how he would fit the tit-bits to the puny mouths, reserving the lengthier links for the seniors – how he would intercept a morsel even in the jaws of some young desperado, declaring it 'must to the pan again to be browned, for it was not fit for a gentleman's eating' – how he would recommend this slice of white bread, or that piece of kissing-crust, to a tender juvenile, advising them all to have a care of cracking their teeth, which were their best patrimony, – how genteelly he would deal about the small ale, as if it were wine, naming the brewer, and protesting, if it were not good, he should lose their custom; with a special recommendation to wipe the lip before drinking. Then we had our toasts – 'The King,' – 'the Cloth,' – which, whether they understood or not, was equally diverting and flattering; – and for a crowning sentiment, which never failed, 'May the Brush supersede the Laurel!' All these, and fifty other fancies, which were rather felt than comprehended by his guests, would he utter, standing upon tables, and prefacing every sentiment with a 'Gentlemen, give me leave to propose so and so,' which was a prodigious comfort to those young orphans; every now and then stuffing into his mouth (for it did not do to be squeamish on these occasions) indiscriminate pieces of those reeking sausages, which pleased them mightily, and was the savouriest part, you may believe, of the entertainment.

> Golden lads and lasses must,
> As chimney-sweepers, come to dust –

JAMES WHITE is extinct, and with him these suppers have long ceased. He carried away with him half the fun of the world when he died – of my world at least. His old clients look for him among the pens; and, missing him, reproach the altered feast of St. Bartholomew, and the glory of Smithfield departed for ever.

Rejoicings Upon the New Year's Coming of Age

The *Old Year* being dead, and the *New Year* coming of age, which he does, by Calendar Law, as soon as the breath is out of the old gentleman's body, nothing would serve the young spark but he must give a dinner upon the occasion, to which all the *Days* in the year were invited. The *Festivals*, whom he deputed as his stewards, were mightily taken with the notion. They had been engaged time out of mind, they said, in providing mirth and good cheer for mortals below; and it was time they should have a taste of their own bounty. It was stiffly debated among them whether the *Fasts* should be admitted. Some said the appearance of such lean, starved guests, with their mortified faces, would pervert the ends of the meeting. But the objection was overruled by *Christmas Day*, who had a design upon *Ash Wednesday* (as you shall hear), and a mighty desire to see how the old Dominie would behave himself in his cups. Only the *Vigils* were requested to come with their lanterns, to light the gentlefolks home at night.

All the *Days* came to their day. Covers were provided for three hundred and sixty-five guests at the principal table; with an occasional knife and fork at the side-board for the *Twenty-Ninth of February*.

I should have told you that cards of invitation had been issued. The carriers were the *Hours*; twelve little, merry, whirligig foot-pages, as you should desire to see, that went all round, and found out the persons invited well enough, with the exception of *Easter Day*, *Shrove Tuesday*, and a few such *Moveables*, who had lately shifted their quarters.

Well, they all met at last, foul *Days*, fine *Days*, all sorts of *Days*, and a rare din they made of it. There was nothing but, Hail! fellow *Day*, – well met – brother *Day* – sister *Day* – only *Lady Day* kept a little on the aloof, and seemed somewhat scornful. Yet some said, *Twelfth Day* cut her out and out, for she came in a tiffany suit, white and gold, like a queen on a frost-cake, all royal, glittering, and *Epiphanous*. The rest came, some in green, some in white – but old *Lent and his family* were not yet out of mourning. Rainy *Days* came in, dripping; and sunshiny *Days* helped them to change their stockings. *Wedding Day* was there in his marriage finery, a little the worse for wear. *Pay Day* came late, as he always does; and *Doomsday* sent word – he might be expected.

April Fool (as my young lord's jester) took upon himself to marshal the guests, and wild work he made with it. It would have posed old Erra Pater to have found out any given *Day* in the year, to erect a scheme upon – good *Days*, bad *Days*, were so shuffled together, to the confounding of all sober horoscopy.

He had stuck the *Twenty-First of June* next to the *Twenty-Second of December*, and the former looked like a Maypole siding a marrow-bone. *Ash Wednesday* got wedged in (as was concerted) betwixt *Christmas* and *Lord Mayor's Days*. Lord! how he laid about him! Nothing but barons of beef and turkeys would go down with him – to the great greasing and detriment of his new sackcloth bib and tucker. And still *Christmas Day* was at his elbow, plying him with the wassail bowl, till he roared, and hiccupp'd, and protested there was no faith in dried ling, but commended it to the devil for a sour, windy, acrimonious, censorious, hy-po-crit-crit-critical mess, and no dish for a gentleman. Then he dipt his fist into the middle of the great custard that stood before his *left hand neighbour*, and daubed his hungry beard all over with it, till you would have taken him for the *Last Day in December*, it so hung in icicles.

At another part of the table, *Shrove Tuesday* was helping the *Second of September* to some cock broth, – which courtesy the latter returned with the delicate thigh of a hen pheasant – so there was no love lost for that matter. The *Last of Lent* was spunging upon *Shrovetide's* pancakes; which *April Fool* perceiving, told him he did well, for pancakes were proper to a *good fry-day*.

In another part, a hubbub arose about the *Thirtieth of January*, who, it seems, being a sour, puritanic character, that thought nobody's meat good or sanctified enough for him, had smuggled into the room a calf's head, which he had had cooked at home for that purpose, thinking to feast thereon incontinently; but as it lay in the dish, *March Manyweathers*, who is a very fine lady, and subject to the meagrims, screamed out there was a 'human head in the platter,' and raved about Herodias' daughter to that degree, that the obnoxious viand was obliged to be removed; nor did she recover her stomach till she had gulped down a *Restorative*, confected of *Oak Apple*, which the merry *Twenty-Ninth of May* always carries about with him for that purpose.

The king's health being called for after this, a notable dispute arose between the *Twelfth of August* (a zealous old Whig gentlewoman) and the *Twenty-Third of April* (a new-fangled lady of the Tory stamp), as to which of them should have the honour to propose it. *August* grew hot upon the matter, affirming time out of mind the prescriptive right to have lain with her, till her rival had basely supplanted her; whom she represented as little better than a *kept* mistress, who went about in *fine clothes*, while she (the legitimate BIRTHDAY) had scarcely a rag, &c.

April Fool, being made mediator, confirmed the right, in the strongest form of words, to the appellant, but decided for peace' sake that the exercise of it should remain with the present possessor. At the same time, he slyly rounded the first lady in the ear, that an action might lie against the Crown for *by-geny*.

It beginning to grow a little duskish, *Candlemas* lustily bawled out for lights, which was opposed by all the *Days*, who protested against burning daylight. Then fair water was handed round in silver ewers, and the *same lady* was observed to take an unusual time in *Washing* herself.

May Day, with that sweetness which is peculiar to her, in a neat speech proposing the health of the founder, crowned her goblet (and by her example the rest of the company) with garlands. This being done, the lordly *New Year*, from the upper end of the table, in a cordial but somewhat lofty tone, returned thanks. He felt proud on an occasion of meeting so many of his worthy father's late tenants, promised to improve their farms, and at the same time to abate (if anything was found unreasonable) in their rents.

At the mention of this, the four *Quarter Days* involuntarily looked at each other, and smiled; *April Fool* whistled to an old tune of 'New Brooms;' and a surly old rebel at the further end of the table (who was discovered to be no other than the *Fifth of November*) muttered out, distinctly enough to be heard by the whole company, words to this effect, that 'when the old one is gone, he is a fool that looks for a better.' Which rudeness of his, the guests resenting, unanimously voted his expulsion; and the malecontent was thrust out neck and heels into the cellar, as the properest place for such a *boutefeu* and firebrand as he had shown himself to be.

Order being restored – the young lord (who, to say truth, had been a little ruffled, and put beside his oratory) in as few, and yet as obliging words as possible, assured them of entire welcome; and, with a graceful turn, singling out poor *Twenty-Ninth of February*, that had sate all this while mumchance at the side-board, begged to couple his health with that of the good company before him – which he drank accordingly; observing that he had not seen his honest face any time these four years – with a number of endearing expressions besides. At the same time, removing the solitary *Day* from the forlorn seat which had been assigned him, he stationed him at his own board, somewhere between the *Greek Calends* and *Latter Lammas*.

Ash Wednesday, being now called upon for a song, with his eyes fast stuck in his head, and as well as the Canary he had swallowed would give him leave, struck up a Carol, which *Christmas Day* had taught him for the nonce; and was followed by the latter, who gave

'Miserere,' in fine style, hitting off the mumping notes and lengthened drawl of *Old Mortification* with infinite humour. *April Fool* swore they had exchanged conditions, but *Good Friday* was observed to look extremely grave; and *Sunday* held her fan before her face that she might not be seen to smile.

Shrove-tide, *Lord Mayor's Day*, and *April Fool*, next joined in a glee –

Which is the properest day to drink?

in which all the *Days* chiming in, made a merry burden.

They next fell to quibbles and conundrums. The question being proposed, who had the greatest number of followers – the *Quarter Days* said, there could be no question as to that; for they had all the creditors in the world dogging their heels. But *April Fool* gave it in favour of the *Forty Days before Easter;* because the debtors in all cases out-numbered the creditors, and they kept *lent* all the year.

All this while *Valentine's Day* kept courting pretty *May*, who sate next him, slipping amorous *billets-doux* under the table, till the *Dog Days* (who are naturally of a warm constitution) began to be jealous, and to bark and rage exceedingly. *April Fool*, who likes a bit of sport above measure, and had some pretensions to the lady besides, as being but a cousin once removed, – clapped and halloo'd them on; and as fast as their indignation cooled, those mad wags, the *Ember Days*, were at it with their bellows, to blow it into a flame; and all was in a ferment; till old Madam *Septuagesima* (who boasts herself the *Mother of the Days*) wisely diverted the conversation with a tedious tale of the lovers which she could reckon when she was young; and of one Master *Rogation Day* in particular, who was for ever putting the *question* to her; but she kept him at a distance, as the chronicle would tell – by which I apprehend she meant the Almanack. Then she rambled on to the *Days that were gone*, the *good old Days*, and so to the *Days before the Flood* – which plainly showed her old head to be little better than crazed and doited.

Day being ended, the *Days* called for their cloaks and great-coats, and took their leaves. *Lord Mayor's Day* went off in a Mist, as usual; *Shortest Day* in a deep black Fog, that wrapt the little gentleman all round like a hedge-hog. Two *Vigils* – so watchmen are called in heaven – saw *Christmas Day* safe home – they had been used to the business before. Another *Vigil* – a stout, sturdy, patrole, called the *Eve of St. Christopher* – seeing *Ash Wednesday* in a condition little better than he should be – e'en whipt him over his shoulders, pick-a-back fashion, and *Old Mortification* went floating home singing –

> On the bat's back do I fly,

and a number of old snatches besides, between drunk and sober; but very few Aves or Penitentiaries (you may believe me) were among them. *Longest Day* set off west-ward in beautiful crimson and gold – the rest, some in one fashion, some in another; but *Valentine* and pretty *May* took their departure together in one of the prettiest silvery twilights a Lover's Day could wish to set in.

Confessions of a Drunkard

Dehortations from the use of strong liquors have been the favourite topic of sober declaimers in all ages, and have been received with abundance of applause by water-drinking critics. But with the patient himself, the man that is to be cured, unfortunately their sound has seldom prevailed. Yet the evil is acknowledged, the remedy simple. Abstain. No force can oblige a man to raise the glass to his head against his will. 'Tis as easy as not to steal, not to tell lies.

Alas! the hand to pilfer, and the tongue to bear false witness, have no constitutional tendency. These are actions indifferent to them. At the first instance of the reformed will, they can be brought off without a murmur. The itching finger is but a figure in speech, and the tongue of the liar can with the same natural delight give forth useful truths with which it has been accustomed to scatter their pernicious contraries. But when a man has commenced sot—

O pause, thou sturdy moralist, thou person of stout nerves and a strong head, whose liver is happily untouched, and ere thy gorge riseth at the *name* which I have written, first learn what the *thing* is; how much of compassion, how much of human allowance, thou mayest virtuously mingle with thy disapprobation. Trample not on the ruins of a man. Exact not, under so terrible a penalty as infamy, a resuscitation from a state of death almost as real as that from which Lazarus rose not but by a miracle.

Begin a reformation, and custom will make it easy. But what if the beginning be dreadful, the first steps not like climbing a mountain but going through fire? what if the whole system must undergo a change violent as that which we conceive of the mutation of form in some insects? what if a process comparable to flaying alive be to be gone through? is the weakness that sinks under such struggles to be confounded with the pertinacity which clings to other vices, which have induced no constitutional necessity, no engagement of the whole victim, body and soul!

I have known one in that state, when he has tried to abstain but for one evening, – though the poisonous potion had long ceased to bring back its first enchantments, though he was sure it would rather deepen his gloom than brighten it, – in the violence of the struggle, and the necessity he has felt of getting rid of the present sensation at any rate, I have known him to scream out, to cry aloud, for the anguish and pain of the strife within him.

Why should I hesitate to declare, that the man of whom I speak is myself? I have no puling apology to make to mankind. I see them all in one way or another deviating from the pure reason. It is to my own nature alone I am accountable for the woe that I have brought upon it.

I believe that there are constitutions, robust heads and iron insides, whom scarce any excesses can hurt; whom brandy (I have seen them drink it like wine), at all events whom wine, taken in ever so plentiful a measure, can do no worse injury to than just to muddle their faculties, perhaps never very pellucid. On them this discourse is wasted. They would but laugh at a weak brother, who, trying his strength with them, and coming off foiled from the contest, would fain persuade them that such agonistic exercises are dangerous. It is to a very different description of persons I speak. It is to the weak, the nervous; to those who feel the want of some artificial aid to raise their spirits in society to what is no more than the ordinary pitch of all around them without it. This is the secret of our drinking. Such must fly the convivial board in the first instance, if they do not mean to sell themselves for term of life.

Twelve years ago I had completed my six-and-twentieth year. I had lived from the period of leaving school to that time pretty much in solitude. My companions were chiefly books, or at most one or two living ones of my own book-loving and sober stamp. I rose early, went to bed betimes, and the faculties which God had given me, I have reason to think, did not rust in me unused.

About that time I fell in with some companions of a different order. They were men of boisterous spirits, sitters up a-nights, disputants, drunken; yet seemed to have something noble about them. We dealt about the wit, or what passes for it after midnight, jovially. Of the quality called fancy I certainly possessed a larger share than my companions. Encouraged by their applause, I set up for a professed joker! I, who of all men am least fitted for such an occupation, having, in addition to the greatest difficulty which I experience at all times of finding words to express my meaning, a natural nervous impediment in my speech!

Reader, if you are gifted with nerves like mine, aspire to any character but that of a wit. When you find a tickling relish upon your tongue disposing you to that sort of conversation, especially if you find a preternatural flow of ideas setting in upon you at the sight of a bottle and fresh glasses, avoid giving way to it as you would fly your greatest destruction. If you cannot crush the power of fancy, or that within you which you mistake for such, divert it, give it some other play. Write an essay, pen a character or description, – but not as I do now, with tears trickling down your cheeks.

To be an object of compassion to friends, of derision to foes; to be suspected by strangers, stared at by fools; to be esteemed dull when you cannot be witty, to be applauded for witty when you know that you have been dull; to be called upon for the extemporaneous exercise of that faculty which no premeditation can give; to be spurred on to efforts which end in contempt; to be set on to provoke mirth which procures the procurer hatred; to give pleasure and be paid with squinting malice; to swallow draughts of life-destroying wine which are to be distilled into airy breath to tickle vain auditors; to mortgage miserable morrows for nights of madness; to waste whole seas of time upon those who pay it back in little inconsiderable drops of grudging applause, – are the wages of buffoonery and death.

Time, which has a sure stroke at dissolving all connexions which have no solider fastening than this liquid cement, more kind to me than my own taste or penetration, at length opened my eyes to the supposed qualities of my first friends. No trace of them is left but in the vices which they introduced, and the habits they infixed. In them my friends survive still, and exercise ample retribution for any supposed infidelity that I may have been guilty of towards them.

My next more immediate companions were and are persons of such intrinsic and felt worth, that though accidentally their acquaintance has proved pernicious to me, I do not know that if the thing were to do over again, I should have the courage to eschew the mischief at the price of forfeiting the benefit. I came to them reeking from the steams of my late over-heated notions of companionship; and the slightest fuel which they unconsciously afforded, was sufficient to feed my old fires into a propensity.

They were no drinkers, but, one from professional habits, and another from a custom derived from his father, smoked tobacco. The devil could not have devised a more subtle trap to re-take a backsliding penitent. The transition, from gulping down draughts of liquid fire to puffing out innocuous blasts of dry smoke, was so like cheating him. But he is too hard for us when we hope to commute. He beats us at barter; and when we think to set off a new failing against an old infirmity, 'tis odds but he puts the trick upon us of two for one. That (comparatively) white devil of tobacco brought with him in the end seven worse than himself.

It were impertinent to carry the reader through all the processes by which, from smoking at first with malt liquor, I took my degrees through thin wines, through stronger wine and water, through small punch, to those juggling compositions, which, under the name of mixed liquors, slur a great deal of brandy or other poison under less and less water continually, until they come next to none, and so to none at all. But it is hateful to disclose the secrets of my Tartarus.

I should repel my readers, from a mere incapacity of believing me, were I to tell them what tobacco has been to me, the drudging service which I have paid, the slavery which I have vowed to it. How, when I have resolved to quit it, a feeling as of ingratitude has started up; how it has put on personal claims and made the demands of a friend upon me. How the reading of it casually in a book, as where Adams takes his whiff in the chimney-corner of some Inn in Joseph Andrews, or Piscator in the Complete Angler breaks his fast upon a morning pipe in that delicate room *Piscatoribus Sacrum*, has in a moment broken down the resistance of weeks. How a pipe was ever in my midnight path before me, till the vision forced me to realise it, – how then its ascending vapours curled, its fragrance lulled, and the thousand delicious ministerings conversant about it, employing every faculty, extracted the sense of pain. How from illuminating it came to darken, from a quick solace it turned to a negative relief, thence to a restlessness and dissatisfaction, thence to a positive misery. How, even now, when the whole secret stands confessed in all its dreadful truth before me, I feel myself linked to it beyond the power of revocation. Bone of my bone –

Persons not accustomed to examine the motives of their actions, to reckon up the countless nails that rivet the chains of habit, or perhaps being bound by none so obdurate as those I have confessed to, may recoil from this as from an overcharged picture. But what short of such a bondage is it, which in spite of protesting friends, a weeping wife, and a reprobating world, chains down many a poor fellow, of no original indisposition to goodness, to his pipe and his pot?

I have seen a print after Correggio, in which three female figures are ministering to a man who sits fast bound at the root of a tree. Sensuality is soothing him, Evil Habit is nailing him to a branch, and Repugnance at the same instant of time is applying a snake to his side. In his face is feeble delight, the recollection of past rather than perception of present pleasures, languid enjoyment of evil with utter imbecility to good, a Sybaritic effeminacy, a submission to bondage, the springs of the will gone down like a broken clock, the sin and the suffering co-instantaneous, or the latter forerunning the former, remorse preceding action – all this represented in one point of time. – When I saw this, I admired the wonderful skill of the painter. But when I went away, I wept, because I thought of my own condition.

Of *that* there is no hope that it should ever change. The waters have gone over me. But out of the black depths, could I be heard, I would cry out to all those who have but set a foot in the perilous flood. Could the youth, to whom the flavour of his first wine is delicious as the opening scenes of life or the entering upon some newly discovered paradise, look into my desolation, and be made to understand what a dreary thing it is when a man shall feel himself going down a precipice with open eyes and a passive will, – to see his destruction and have no power to stop it, and yet to feel it all the way emanating from himself; to perceive all goodness emptied out of him, and yet not to be able to forget a time when it was otherwise; to bear about the piteous spectacle of his own self-ruins: – could he see my fevered eye, feverish with last night's drinking, and feverishly looking for this night's repetition of the folly; could he feel the body of the death out of which I cry hourly with feebler and feebler outcry to be delivered, – it were enough to make him dash the sparkling beverage to the earth in all the pride of its mantling temptation; to make him clasp his teeth,

and not undo 'em
To suffer WET DAMNATION to run thro' 'em.

Yea, but (methinks I hear somebody object) if sobriety be that fine thing you would have us to understand, if the comforts of a cool brain are to be preferred to that state of heated excitement which you describe and deplore, what hinders in your instance that you do not return to those habits from which you would induce others never to swerve? if the blessing be worth preserving, is it not worth recovering?

Recovering! – O if a wish could transport me back to those days of youth, when a draught from the next clear spring could slake any heats which summer suns and youthful exercise had power to stir up in the blood, how gladly would I return to thee, pure element, the drink of children, and of child-like holy hermit! In my dreams I can sometimes fancy thy cool refreshment purling over my burning tongue. But my waking stomach rejects it.

That which refreshes innocence only makes me sick and faint.

But is there no middle way betwixt total abstinence and the excess which kills you? – For your sake, reader, and that you may never attain to my experience, with pain I must utter the dreadful truth, that there is none, none that I can find. In my stage of habit (I speak not of habits less confirmed – for some of them I believe the advice to be most prudential) in the stage which I have reached, to stop short of that measure which is sufficient to draw on torpor and sleep, the benumbing apoplectic sleep of the drunkard, is to have taken none at all. The pain of the self-denial is all one. And what that is, I had rather the reader should believe on my credit, than know from his own trial. He will come to know it, whenever he shall arrive in that state, in which, paradoxical as it may appear, *reason shall only visit him through intoxication:* for it is a fearful truth, that the intellectual faculties by repeated acts of intemperance may be driven from their orderly sphere of action, their clear daylight ministeries, until they shall be brought at last to depend, for the faint manifestation of their departing energies, upon the returning periods of the fatal madness to which they owe their devastation. The drinking man is never less himself than during his sober intervals. Evil is so far his good.*

* When poor M— painted his last picture, with a pencil in one trembling hand, and a glass of brandy and water in the other, his fingers owed the comparative steadiness with which they were enabled to go through their task in an imperfect manner, to a temporary firmness derived from a repetition of practices, the general effect of which had shaken both them and him so terribly.

Behold me then, in the robust period of life, reduced to imbecility and decay. Hear me count my gains, and the profits which I have derived from the midnight cup.

Twelve years ago I was possessed of a healthy frame of mind and body. I was never strong, but I think my constitution (for a weak one) was as happily exempt from the tendency to any malady as it was possible to be. I scarce knew what it was to ail anything. Now, except when I am losing myself in a sea of drink, I am never free from those uneasy sensations in head and stomach, which are so much worse to bear than any definite pains or aches.

At that time I was seldom in bed after six in the morning, summer and winter. I awoke refreshed, and seldom without some merry thoughts in my head, or some piece of a song to welcome the new-born day. Now, the first feeling which besets me, after stretching out the hours of recumbence to their last possible extent, is a forecast of the wearisome day that lies before me, with a secret wish that I could have lain on still, or never awaked.

Life itself, my waking life, has much of the confusion, the trouble, and obscure perplexity, of an ill dream. In the day time I stumble upon dark mountains.

Business, which, though never very particularly adapted to my nature, yet as something of necessity to be gone through, and therefore best undertaken with cheerfulness, I used to enter upon with some degree of alacrity, now wearies, affrights, perplexes me. I fancy all sorts of discouragements, and am ready to give up an occupation which gives me bread, from a harassing conceit of incapacity. The slightest commission given me by a friend, or any small duty which I have to perform for myself, as giving orders to a tradesman, &c. haunts me as a labour impossible to be got through. So much the springs of action are broken.

The same cowardice attends me in all my intercourse with mankind. I dare not promise that a friend's honour, or his cause, would be safe in my keeping, if I were put to the expense of any manly resolution in defending it. So much the springs of moral action are deadened within me.

My favourite occupations in times past now cease to entertain. I can do nothing readily. Application for ever so short a time kills me. This poor abstract of my condition was penned at long intervals, with scarcely any attempt at connexion of thought, which is now difficult to me.

The noble passages which formerly delighted me in history or poetic fiction, now only draw a few weak tears, allied to dotage. My broken and dispirited nature seems to sink before anything great and admirable.

I perpetually catch myself in tears, for any cause, or none. It is inexpressible how much this infirmity adds to a sense of shame, and a general feeling of deterioration.

These are some of the instances, concerning which I can say with truth, that it was not always so with me.

Shall I lift up the veil of my weakness any further? – or is this disclosure sufficient?

I am a poor nameless egotist, who have no vanity to consult by these Confessions. I know not whether I shall be laughed at or heard seriously. Such as they are, I commend them to the reader's attention, if he find his own case any way touched. I have told him what I am come to. Let him stop in time.

Elia on His 'Confessions of a Drunkard'

Many are the sayings of Elia, painful and frequent his lucubrations, set forth for the most part (such his modesty!) without a name; scattered about in obscure periodicals and forgotten miscellanies. From the dust of some of these it is our intention occasionally to revive a tract or two that shall seem worthy of a better fate, especially at a time like the present, when the pen of our industrious contributor, engaged in a laborious digest of his recent Continental tour, may haply want the leisure to expatiate in more miscellaneous speculations. We have been induced, in the first instance, to reprint a thing which he put forth in a friend's volume some years since, entitled 'The Confessions of a Drunkard,' seeing that Messieurs the Quarterly Reviewers have chosen to embellish their last dry pages with fruitful quotations therefrom; adding, from their peculiar brains, the gratuitous affirmation, that they have reason to believe that the describer (in his delineations of a drunkard, forsooth!) partly sat for his own picture. The truth is, that our friend had been reading among the essays of a contemporary, who has perversely been confounded with him, a paper in which Edax (or the Great Eater) humorously complaineth of an inordinate appetite; and it struck him that a better paper – of deeper interest and wider usefulness – might be made out of the imagined experiences of a Great Drinker.

Accordingly he set to work, and, with that mock fervour and counterfeit earnestness with which he is too apt to over-realise his descriptions, has given us a frightful picture indeed, but no more resembling the man Elia than the fictitious Edax may be supposed to identify itself with Mr. L., its author. It is indeed a compound extracted out of his long observations of the effects of drinking upon all the world about him; and this accumulated mass of misery he hath centred (as the custom is with judicious essayists) in a single figure. We deny not that a portion of his own experiences may have passed into the picture; (as who, that is not a washy fellow, but must at some times have felt the after-operation of a too-generous cup?) but then how heightened! how exaggerated! how little within the sense of the Review, where a part, in their slanderous usage, must be understood to stand for the whole! But it is useless to expostulate with this Quarterly slime, brood of Nilus, watery heads with hearts of jelly, spawned under the sign of Aquarius, incapable of Bacchus, and therefore cold, washy, spiteful, bloodless. Elia shall string them up one day, and show their colours, – or rather, how colourless and vapid the whole fry, – when he putteth forth his long-promised, but unaccountably hitherto delayed, 'Confessions of a Water-drinker.'

Popular Fallacies

VI. – THAT ENOUGH IS AS GOOD AS A FEAST

NOT a man, woman, or child, in ten miles round Guildhall, who really believes this saying. The inventor of it did not believe it himself. It was made in revenge by somebody, who was disappointed of a regale. It is a vile cold-scrag-of-mutton sophism; a lie palmed upon the palate, which knows better things. If nothing else could be said for a feast, this is sufficient, that from the superflux there is usually something left for the next day. Morally interpreted, it belongs to a class of proverbs which have a tendency to make us undervalue *money*. Of this cast are those notable observations, that money is not health; riches cannot purchase everything; the metaphor which makes gold to be mere muck, with the morality which traces fine clothing to the sheep's back, and denounces pearl as the unhandsome excretion of an oyster. Hence, too, the phrase which imputes dirt to acres – a sophistry so barefaced, that even the literal sense of it is true only in a wet season. This, and abundance of similar sage saws assuming to inculcate *content*, we verily believe to have been the invention of some cunning borrower, who had designs upon the purse of his wealthier neighbour, which he could only hope to carry by force of these verbal jugglings. Translate any one of these sayings out of the artful metonymy which envelopes it, and the trick is apparent. Goodly legs and shoulders of mutton, exhilarating cordials, books, pictures, the opportunities of seeing foreign countries, independence, heart's ease, a man's own time to himself, are not *muck* – however we may be pleased to scandalize with that appellation the faithful metal that provides them for us.

Edax on Appetite

To the Editor of 'The Reflector'

MR. REFLECTOR, – I am going to lay before you a case of the most iniquitous persecution that ever poor devil suffered.

You must know, then, that I have been visited with a calamity ever since my birth. How shall I mention it without offending delicacy? Yet out it must. My sufferings, then, have all arisen from a most inordinate appetite —

Not for wealth, not for vast possessions, – then might I have hoped to find a cure in some of those precepts of philosophers or poets, – those verba et voces which Horace speaks of: –

> quibus hunc lenire dolorem
> Possis, et magnam morbi deponere partem;

not for glory, not for fame, not for applause, – for against this disease, too, he tells us there are certain piacula, or, as Pope has chosen to render it,

> rhymes, which fresh and fresh applied,
> Will cure the arrant'st puppy of his pride;

nor yet for pleasure, properly so called: the strict and virtuous lessons which I received in early life from the best of parents, – a pious clergyman of the Church of

England, now no more, – I trust have rendered me sufficiently secure on that side:—

No, Sir, for none of these things; but an appetite, in its coarsest and least metaphorical sense, – an appetite for *food*.

The exorbitancies of my arrow-root and pappish days I cannot go back far enough to remember; only I have been told that my mother's constitution not admitting of my being nursed at home, the woman who had the care of me for that purpose used to make most extravagant demands for my pretended excesses in that kind; which my parents, rather than believe anything unpleasant of me, chose to impute to the known covetousness and mercenary disposition of that sort of people. This blindness continued on their part after I was sent for home, up to the period when it was thought proper, on account of my advanced age, that I should mix with other boys more unreservedly than I had hitherto done. I was accordingly sent to boarding-school.

Here the melancholy truth became too apparent to be disguised. The prying republic of which a great school consists soon found me out; there was no shifting the blame any longer upon other people's shoulders, – no good-natured maid to take upon herself the enormities of which I stood accused in the article of bread and butter, besides the crying sin of stolen ends of puddings, and cold pies strangely missing. The truth was but too manifest in my looks, – in the evident signs of inanition which I exhibited after the fullest meals, in spite of the double allowance which my master was privately instructed by my kind parents to give me. The sense of the ridiculous, which is but too much alive in grown persons, is tenfold more active and alert in boys. Once detected, I was the constant butt of their arrows, – the mark against which every puny leveller directed his little shaft of scorn. The very Graduses and Thesauruses were raked for phrases to pelt me with by the tiny pedants. Ventri natus, – Ventri deditus, – Vesana gula, – Escarum gurges, – Dapibus indulgens, – Non dans fræna gulæ, – Sectans lautæ fercula mensæ, resounded wheresoever I passed. I led a weary life, suffering the penalties of guilt for that which was no crime, but only following the blameless dictates of nature. The remembrance of those childish reproaches haunts me yet oftentimes in my dreams. My school-days come again, and the horror I used to feel, when, in some silent corner, retired from the notice of my unfeeling playfellows, I have sat to mumble the solitary slice of gingerbread allotted me by the bounty of considerate friends, and have ached at heart because I could not spare a portion of it, as I saw other boys do, to some favourite boy; for if I know my own heart, I was never selfish, – never possessed a luxury which I did not hasten to communicate to others; but my food, alas! was none; it was an indispensable necessary; I could as soon have spared the blood in my veins, as have parted that with my companions.

Well, no one stage of suffering lasts for ever: we should grow reconciled to it at length, I suppose, if it did. The miseries of my school-days had their end; I was once more restored to the paternal dwelling. The affectionate solicitude of my parents was directed to the good-natured purpose of concealing, even from myself, the infirmity which haunted me. I was continually told that I was growing, and the appetite I displayed was humanely represented as being nothing more than a symptom and an effect of that. I used even to be complimented upon it. But this temporary fiction could not endure above a year or two. I ceased to grow, but, alas! I did not cease my demands for alimentary sustenance.

Those times are long since past, and with them have ceased to exist the fond concealment – the indulgent blindness – the delicate overlooking – the compassionate fiction. I and my infirmity are left exposed and bare to the broad, unwinking eye of the world, which nothing can elude. My meals are scanned, my mouthfuls weighed in a balance; that which appetite demands is set down to the account of gluttony, – a sin which my whole soul abhors – nay, which Nature herself has put it out of my power to commit. I am constitutionally disenabled from that vice; for how can he be guilty of excess who never can get enough? Let them cease, then, to watch my plate; and leave off their ungracious comparisons of it to the seven baskets of fragments, and the supernaturally-replenished cup of old Baucis: and be thankful that their more phlegmatic stomachs, not their virtue, have saved them from the like reproaches. I do not see that any of them desist from eating till the holy rage of hunger, as some one calls it, is supplied. Alas! I am doomed to stop short of that continence.

What am I to do? I am by disposition inclined to conviviality and the social meal. I am no gourmand: I require no dainties: I should despise the board of Heliogabalus, except for its long sitting. Those vivacious, long-continued meals of the latter Romans, indeed, I justly envy; but the kind of fare which the Curii and Dentati put up with, I could be content with. Dentatus I have been called, among other unsavoury jests. Doublemeal is another name which my acquaintance have palmed upon me, for an innocent piece of policy which I put in practice for some time without being found out; which was – going the round of my friends, beginning with the most primitive feeders among them, who take their dinner about one o'clock, and so successively dropping in upon the next and the next, till by the time I got among my more fashionable intimates, whose hour was six or seven, I have nearly made up the body of a just and complete meal (as I reckon it), without taking more than one dinner (as they account of dinners) at one person's house. Since I have been found out, I endeavour to make up by a damper, as I call it, at home, before I go out. But alas! with me, increase of appetite truly grows by what it feeds on. What is peculiarly offensive to me at those dinner-parties is, the senseless custom of cheese, and the dessert afterwards. I have a rational antipathy to the former; and for fruit, and those other vain vegetable substitutes for meat (meat, the only legitimate aliment for human creatures since the Flood, as I take it to be deduced from that permission, or ordinance rather, given to Noah and his descendants), I hold them in perfect contempt. Hay for horses. I remember a pretty apologue, which Mandeville tells, very much to this purpose, in his Fable of the Bees: – He brings in a Lion arguing with a Merchant, who had ventured to expostulate with this king of beasts upon his violent methods of feeding. The Lion thus retorts: – 'Savage I am; but no creature can be called cruel but what either by malice or insensibility extinguishes his natural pity. The Lion was born without compassion; we follow the instinct of our nature; the gods have appointed us to live upon the waste and spoil of other animals, and as long as we can meet with dead ones, we never hunt after the living; 'tis only man, mischievous man, that can make death a sport. Nature taught your stomach to crave nothing but vegetables. – (Under favour of the Lion, if he meant to assert this universally of mankind, it is not true. However, what he says presently is very sensible.) – Your violent fondness to change, and greater eagerness after novelties, have prompted you to the destruction of animals without justice or necessity. The Lion has a ferment within him, that consumes the toughest skin and hardest bones, as well as the flesh of all animals, without exception. Your squeamish stomach, in which the digestive heat is weak and inconsiderable, won't so much as admit of the most tender parts of them, unless above half the concoction has been performed by artificial fire beforehand; and yet what animal have you spared, to satisfy the caprices of a languid appetite? Languid, I say; for what is man's hunger if compared with the Lion's? Yours, when it is at the worst, makes you faint; mine makes me mad: oft have I tried with roots and herbs to allay the violence of it, but in vain; nothing but large quantities of flesh can any ways appease it.' – Allowing for the Lion not having a prophetic instinct to take in every lusus naturæ that was possible of the human appetite, he was, generally speaking, in the right; and the Merchant was so impressed with his argument that, we are told, he replied not, but fainted away. O, Mr. Reflector, that I were not obliged to add, that the creature who thus argues was but a type of me! Miserable man! *I am that Lion!* 'Oft have I tried with roots and herbs to allay that violence, but in vain; nothing but ——'

Those tales which are renewed as often as the editors of papers want to fill up a space in their unfeeling columns, of great eaters, – people that devour whole geese and legs of mutton *for wagers*, – are sometimes attempted to be drawn to a parallel with my case. This wilful confounding of motives and circumstances, which make all the difference of moral or immoral in actions, just suits the sort of talent which some of my acquaintance pride themselves upon. *Wagers!* – I thank Heaven, I was never mercenary, nor could consent to prostitute a gift (though but a left-handed one) of nature, to the enlarging of my worldly substance; prudent as the necessities, which that fatal gift have involved me in, might have made such a prostitution to appear in the eyes of an indelicate world.

Rather let me say, that to the satisfaction of that talent which was given me, I have been content to sacrifice no common expectations; for such I had from an old lady, a near relation of our family, in whose good graces I had the fortune to stand, till one fatal evening ——. You have seen, Mr. Reflector, if you have ever passed your time much in country towns, the kind of suppers which elderly ladies in those places have lying *in petto* in an adjoining parlour, next to that where they are entertaining their periodically-invited coevals with cards and muffins. The cloth is usually spread some half-hour before the final rubber is decided, whence they adjourn to sup upon what may emphatically be called *nothing;* – a sliver of ham, purposely contrived to be transparent to show the china-dish through it, neighbouring a slip of invisible brawn, which abuts upon something they call a tartlet, as that is bravely supported by an atom of marmalade, flanked in its turn by a grain of potted beef, with a power of such dishlings, *minims of hospitality*, spread in defiance of human nature, or rather with an utter ignorance of what it demands. Being engaged at one of these card-parties, I was obliged to go a little before *supper time* (as they facetiously called the point of time in which they are taking these shadowy refections), and the old lady, with a sort of fear shining through the smile of courteous hospitality that beamed in her countenance, begged me to step into the next room and take something before I went out into the cold, – a proposal which lay not in my nature to deny. Indignant at the airy prospect I saw before me, I set to, and in a trice despatched the whole meal intended for eleven persons, – fish, flesh, fowl, pastry, – to the sprigs of garnishing parsley, and the last fearful custard that quaked upon the board. I need not describe the consternation, when in due time the dowagers adjourned from their cards. Where was the supper? – and the servants' answer, Mr. — had eat it all. – That freak, however, jested me out of a good three hundred pounds a year, which I afterwards was informed for a certainty the old lady meant to leave me. I mention it not in illustration of the unhappy faculty which I am possessed of; for any unlucky wag of a schoolboy, with a tolerable appetite, could have done as much without feeling any hurt after it, – only that you may judge whether I am a man likely to set my talent to sale, or to require the pitiful stimulus of a wager.

I have read in Pliny, or in some author of that stamp, of a reptile in Africa, whose venom is of that hot, destructive quality, that wheresoever it fastens its tooth, the whole substance of the animal that has been bitten in a few seconds is reduced to dust, crumbles away, and absolutely disappears: it is called, from this quality, the Annihilator. Why am I forced to seek, in all the most prodigious and portentous facts of Natural History, for creatures typical of myself? *I am that snake, that Annihilator:* 'wherever I fasten, in a few seconds —'

O happy sick men, that are groaning under the want of that very thing the excess of which is my torment! O fortunate, too fortunate, if you knew your happiness, invalids! What would I not give to exchange this fierce concoctive and digestive heat, – this rabid fury which vexes me, which tears and torments me, – for your quiet, mortified, hermit-like, subdued, and sanctified stomachs, your cool, chastened inclinations, and coy desires for food!

To what unhappy figuration of the parts intestine I owe this unnatural craving, I must leave to the anatomists and the physicians to determine: they, like the rest of the world, have doubtless their eye upon me; and as I have been cut up alive by the sarcasms of my friends, so I shudder when I contemplate the probability that this animal frame, when its restless appetites shall have ceased their importunity, may be cut up also (horrible suggestion!) to determine in what system of solids or fluids this original sin of my constitution lay lurking. What work will they make with their acids and alkalines, their serums and coagulums, effervescences, viscous matter, bile, chyle, and acrimonious juices, to explain that cause which Nature, who willed the effect to punish me for my sins, may no less have determined to keep in the dark from them, to punish them for their presumption!

You may ask, Mr. Reflector, to what purpose is my appeal to you; what can you do for me? Alas! I know too well that my case is out of the reach of advice, – out of the reach of consolation. But it is some relief to the wounded heart to impart its tale of misery; and some of my acquaintance, who may read my case in your pages under a borrowed name, may be induced to give it a more humane consideration than I could ever yet obtain from them under my own. Make them, if possible, to *reflect*, that an original peculiarity of constitution is no crime; that not that which goes into the mouth desecrates a man, but that which comes out of it, – such as sarcasm, bitter jests, mocks and taunts, and ill-natured observations; and let them consider, if there be such things (which we have all heard of) as Pious Treachery, Innocent Adultery, &c., whether there may not be also such a thing as Innocent Gluttony.

I shall only subscribe myself,
Your afflicted servant,
EDAX.

Hospita on the Immoderate Indulgence of the Pleasures of the Palate

To the Editor of 'The Reflector'

MR. REFLECTOR, – My husband and I are fond of company, and being in easy circumstances, we are seldom without a party to dinner two or three days in a week. The utmost cordiality has hitherto prevailed at our meetings; but there is a young gentleman, a near relation of my husband's, that has lately come among us, whose preposterous behaviour bids fair, if not timely checked, to disturb our tranquillity. He is too great a favourite with my husband in other respects, for me to remonstrate with him in any other than this distant way. A letter printed in your publication may catch his eye; for he is a great reader, and makes a point of seeing all the new things that come out. Indeed, he is by no means deficient in understanding. My husband says that he has a good deal of wit; but for my part I cannot say I am any judge of that, having seldom observed him open his mouth except for purposes very foreign to conversation. In short, Sir, this young gentleman's failing is, an immoderate indulgence of his palate. The first time he dined with us, he thought it necessary to extenuate the length of time he kept the dinner on the table, by declaring that he had taken a very long walk in the morning, and came in fasting; but as that excuse could not serve above once or twice at most, he has latterly dropped the mask altogether, and chosen to appear in his own proper colours without reserve or apology.

You cannot imagine how unpleasant his conduct has become. His way of staring at the dishes as they are brought in, has absolutely something immodest in it: it is like the stare of an impudent man of fashion at a fine woman, when she first comes into a room. I am positively in pain for the dishes, and cannot help thinking they have consciousness, and will be put out of countenance, he treats them so like what they are not.

Then again he makes no scruple of keeping a joint of meat on the table, after the cheese and fruit are brought in, till he has what he calls *done with it*. Now how awkward this looks, where there are ladies, you may judge, Mr. Reflector, – how it disturbs the order and comfort of a meal. And yet I always make a point of helping him first, contrary to all good manners, – before any of my female friends are helped, – that he may avoid this very error. I wish he would eat before he comes out.

What makes his proceedings more particularly offensive at our house is, that my husband, though out of common politeness he is obliged to set dishes of animal food before his visitors, yet himself and his whole family, (myself included) feed entirely on vegetables. We have a theory, that animal food is neither wholesome nor natural to man; and even vegetables we refuse to eat until they have undergone the operation of fire, in consideration of those numberless little living creatures which the glass helps us to detect in every fibre of the plant or root before it be dressed. On the same theory we boil our water, which is our only drink, before we suffer it to come to table. Our children are perfect little Pythagoreans: it would do you good to see them in their nursery, stuffing their dried fruits, figs, raisins, and *milk*, which is the only approach to animal food which is allowed. They have no notion how the substance of a creature that ever had life can become food for another creature. A beef-steak is an absurdity to them; a mutton-chop, a solecism in terms; a cutlet, a word absolutely without any meaning; a butcher is nonsense, except so far as it is taken for a man who delights in blood, or a hero. In this happy state of innocence we have kept their minds, not allowing them to go into the kitchen, or to hear of any preparations for the dressing of animal food, or even to know that such things are practised. But as a state of ignorance is incompatible with a certain age, and as my eldest girl, who is ten years old next Midsummer, must shortly be introduced into the world and sit at table with us, where she will see some things which will shock all her received notions, I have been endeavouring by little and little to break her mind, and prepare it for the disagreeable impressions which must be forced upon it. The first hint I gave her upon the subject, I could see her recoil from it with the same horror with which we listen to a tale of Anthropophagism; but she has gradually grown more reconciled to it, in some measure, from my telling her that it was the custom of the world, – to which, however senseless, we must submit, so far as we could do it with innocence, not to give offence; and she has shown so much strength of mind on other occasions, which I have no doubt is owing to the calmness and serenity superinduced by her diet, that I am in good hopes when the proper season for her *début* arrives, she may be brought to endure the sight of a roasted chicken or a dish of sweet-breads for the first time without fainting. Such being the nature of our little household, you may guess what inroads into the economy of it, – what revolutions and turnings of things upside down, the example of such a feeder as Mr. — is calculated to produce.

I wonder, at a time like the present, when the scarcity of every kind of food is so painfully acknowledged, that *shame* has no effect upon him. Can he have read Mr. Malthus's Thoughts on the Ratio of Food to Population? Can he think it reasonable that one man should consume the sustenance of many?

The young gentleman has an agreeable air and person, such as are not unlikely to recommend him on the score of matrimony. But his fortune is not over large; and what prudent young woman would think of embarking hers with a man who would bring three or four mouths (or what is equivalent to them) into a family? She might as reasonably choose a widower in the same circumstances, with three or four children.

I cannot think who he takes after. His father and mother, by all accounts, were very moderate eaters; only I have heard that the latter swallowed her victuals very fast, and the former had a tedious custom of sitting long at his meals. Perhaps he takes after both.

I wish you would turn this in your thoughts, Mr. Reflector, and give us your ideas on the subject of excessive eating, and, particularly, of animal food.

HOSPITA.

The Months

Rummaging over the contents of an old stall at a half *book*, half *old iron shop*, in an alley leading from Wardour-street to Soho-square yesterday, I lit upon a ragged duodecimo, which had been the strange delight of my infancy, and which I had lost sight of for more than forty years: – the 'QUEEN-LIKE CLOSET, or RICH CABINET'; written by Hannah Woolly, and printed for R. C. and T. S. 1681; being an abstract of receipts in cookery, confectionery, cosmetics, needlework, morality, and all such branches of what were then considered as female accomplishments. The price demanded was sixpence, which the owner (a little squab duodecimo of a character himself) enforced with the assurance that his 'own mother should not have it for a farthing less.' On my demurring at this extraordinary assertion, the dirty little vendor re-enforced his assertion with a sort of oath, which seemed more than the occasion demanded: 'and now (said he) I have put my soul to it.' Pressed by so solemn an asseveration, I could no longer resist a demand which seemed to set me, however unworthy, upon a level with his dearest relations; and depositing a tester, I bore away the tattered prize in triumph. I remembered a gorgeous description of the twelve months of the year, which I thought would be a fine substitute for those poetical descriptions of them which your *Every-Day Book* had nearly exhausted out of Spenser. This will be a treat, thought I, for friend HONE. To memory they seemed no less fantastic and splendid than the other. But, what are the mistakes of childhood! – on reviewing them, they turned out to be only a set of commonplace receipts for working the seasons, months, heathen gods and goddesses, etc., in *samplers*! Yet as an instance of the homely occupations of our great-grandmothers, they may be amusing to some readers: 'I have seen,' says the notable Hannah Woolly, 'such Ridiculous things done in work, as it is an abomination to any Artist to behold. As for example: You may find in some Pieces, *Abraham* and *Sarah*, and many other Persons of Old time, Cloathed as they go now-a-daies, and truly sometimes worse; for they most resemble the Pictures on Ballads. Let all Ingenious Women have regard, that when they work any Image, to represent it aright. First, let it be Drawn well, and then observe the Directions which are given by Knowing Men. I do assure you, I never durst work any Scripture-Story without informing my self from the Ground of it; nor any other Story, or single Person, without informing my self both of the Visage and Habit; As followeth.

'If you work *Jupiter, the Imperial feigned God*, He must have long, Black-Curled hair, a Purple Garment trimmed with Gold, and sitting upon a Golden Throne, with bright yellow Clouds about him.'

THE TWELVE MONTHS OF THE YEAR

March. Is drawn in Tawny, with a fierce aspect, a Helmet upon his head, and leaning on a Spade; and a Basket of Garden Seeds in his Left hand, and in his Right hand the Sign of *Aries*; and Winged.

April. A Young Man in Green, with a Garland of Mirtle and Hawthorn-buds; Winged; in one hand Primroses and Violets, in the other the Sign *Taurus*.

May. With a Sweet and lovely Countenance; clad in a Robe of White and Green, embroidered with several Flowres, upon his Head a garland of all manner of Roses; on the one hand a Nightingale, in the other a Lute. His sign must be *Gemini*.

June. In a Mantle of dark Grass green; upon his Head a garland of Bents, Kings-Cups, and Maidenhair; in his Left hand an Angle, with a box of Cantharides; in his Right, the Sign *Cancer*; and upon his arms a Basket of seasonable Fruits.

July. In a Jacket of light Yellow, eating Cherries; with his Face and Bosom Sun-burnt; on his Head a wreath of Centaury and wild Tyme; a Scythe on his shoulder, and a bottle at his girdle; carrying the Sign *Leo*.

August. A Young Man of fierce and Cholerick aspect, in a Flame-coloured Garment; upon his Head a garland of Wheat and Rye, upon his Arm a Basket of all manner of ripe Fruits, at his Belt a Sickle. His Sign *Virgo*.

September. A merry and chereful Countenance, in a Purple Robe, upon his Head a Wreath of red and white Grapes, in his Left hand a handful of Oats, withal carrying a Horn of Plenty, full of all manner of ripe Fruits; in his Right hand the Sign *Libra*.

October. In a Garment of Yellow and Carnation, upon his head a garland of Oak-leaves with Akorns, in his Right hand the Sign *Scorpio*, in his Left hand a Basket of Medlars, Services, and Chestnuts; and any other Fruits then in Season.

November. In a Garment of Changeable Green and Black, upon his Head a garland of Olives, with the Fruit in his Left hand, Bunches of Parsnips and Turnips in his Right. His Sign *Sagittarius*.

December. A horrid and fearful aspect, clad in Irish-Rags, or coarse Freez girt unto him, upon his Head three or four Night-Caps, and over them a Turkish Turbant; his Nose red, his Mouth and Beard clog'd with Isicles, at his back a bundle of Holly, Ivy, or Mistletoe, holding in fur'd Mittens the Sign of *Capricornus*.

January. Clad all in White, as the Earth looks with the Snow, blowing his nails; in his Left Arm a Bilet, the Sign *Aquarius* standing by his side.

February. Cloathed in a dark Skie-colour, carrying in his Right hand the Sign *Pisces*.

The following receipt, *'To dress up a Chimney very fine for the Summer time, as I have done many, and they have been liked very well,'* may not be unprofitable to the housewives of this century.

'First, take a pack-thred, and fasten it even to the inner part of the Chimney, so high as that you can see no higher as you walk up and down the House; you must drive in several Nails to hold up all your work; then get a good store of old green Moss from Trees, and melt an equal proportion of Bees-wax and Rosin together, and while it is hot, dip the wrong ends of the Moss in it, and presently clap it upon your pack-thred, and press it down hard with your hand; you must make hast, else it will cool before you can fasten it, and then it will fall down; do so all around where the pack-thred goes; and the next row you must joyn to that, so that it may seem all in one; thus do till you have finished it down to the bottom: then take some other kind of Moss, of a whitish-colour and stiff, and of several sorts or kinds, and place that upon the other, here and there carelessly, and in some places put a good deal, and some a little; then any kind of fine Snail-shels, in which the Snails are dead, and little Toad stools, which are very old, and look like Velvet, or *any other thing that is old and pretty*; place it here and there as your fancy serves, and fasten all with Wax and Rosin. Then for the Hearth of your Chimney, you may lay some Orpan-sprigs in order all over, and it will grow as it lies; and according to the Season, get what flowers you can, and stick in as if they grew, and a few sprigs of Sweet-Bryer: the Flowers you must renew every Week; but the Moss will last all the Summer, till it will be time to make a fire; and the Orpan will last near two Months. A Chimney thus done doth grace a Room exceedingly.'

One phrase in the above should particularly recommend it to such of your female readers, as, in the nice language of the day, have done growing some time: 'little toad-stools, etc. and any thing that is *old and pretty*.' Was ever antiquity so smoothed over? The culinary recipes have nothing remarkable in them, except the costliness of them. Every thing (to the meanest meats) is sopped in claret, steeped in claret, basted with claret, as if claret were as cheap as ditch water. I remember Bacon recommends opening a turf or two in your garden walks, and pouring into each a bottle of claret, to recreate the sense of smelling, being no less grateful than beneficial. We hope the chancellor of the exchequer will attend to this in his next reduction of French wines, that we may once more water our gardens with right Bourdeaux. The medical recipes are as whimsical as they are cruel. Our ancestors were not at all effeminate on this head. Modern sentimentalists would shrink at a cock plucked and bruised in a mortar alive, to make a cullis; or a live mole baked in an oven (*be sure it be alive*) to make a powder for consumption. – But the whimsicalest of all are the directions to servants – (for this little book is a compendium of all duties,) – the footman is seriously admonished not to stand lolling against his master's chair, while he waits at table; for 'to lean on a chair, when they wait, is a particular favour shown to any superior servant, as the chief gentleman, or the waiting woman when she rises from the table.' Also he must not 'hold the plates before his mouth to be defiled with his breath, nor touch them on the right [inner] side.' Surely Swift must have seen this little treatise.

Hannah concludes with the following address, by which the self-estimate which she formed of her usefulness, may be calculated:

> *Ladies*, I hope you're pleas'd, and so shall I,
> If what I've writ, you may be gainers by:
> If not; it is your fault, it is not mine,
> Your benefit in this I do design.
> Much labour and much time it hath me cost,

Therefore I beg, let none of it be lost.
The money you shall pay for this my book,
You'll not repent of, when in it you look.
No more at present to you I shall say,
But wish you all the happiness I may.

H. W.

London Fogs

In a well mix'd Metropolitan Fog, there is something substantial and satisfying – you can feel what you breathe, and see it too. It is like breathing water, as we may fancy fishes do. And then the taste of it, when dashed with a fine season of sea-coal smoke, is far from insipid.

It is also meat and drink at the same time; something between egg-flip and *Omelette soufflée*, but much more digestible than either. Not that I would recommend it medicinally – especially to persons that have queasy stomachs, delicate nerves and afflicted with bile; but for persons of a good robust habit of body, and not dainty withal (which such, by the by, never are,) there is nothing better in its way. And it wraps you all round like a cloak, too – a patent waterproof one, which no rain ever penetrated. No; I maintain that a real London Fog is a thing not to be sneezed at – if you can help it.

Mem. – As many spurious imitations of the above are abroad, such as Scotch Mists, and the like, which are no less deleterious than disagreeable, please to ask for the 'true London particular,' as manufactured by Thames, Coal Gas, Smoke, Steam and Co. – None others are genuine.

Thoughts on Presents of Game, etc.

> We love to have our friend in the country sitting thus at our table *by proxy*; to apprehend his presence (though a hundred miles may be between us) by a turkey, whose goodly aspect reflects to us his 'plump corpusculum'; to taste him in grouse or woodcock; to feel him gliding down in the toast peculiar to the latter; to concorporate him in a slice of Canterbury brawn. This is indeed to have him within ourselves; to know him intimately; such participation is methinks *unitive*, as the old theologians phrase it. – *Last Essays of Elia*.

Elia presents his acknowledgments to his 'Correspondent Unknown,' for a basket of prodigiously fine game. He takes for granted that so amiable a character must be a reader of the *Athenæum*. Else he had meditated a notice in *The Times*. Now if this friend had consulted the Delphic oracle for a present suited to the palate of Elia, he could not have hit upon a morsel so acceptable. The birds he is barely thankful for; pheasants are poor *fowls* disguised in fine feathers. But a hare roasted hard and brown – with gravy and melted butter! – old Mr. Chambers, the sensible clergyman in Warwickshire, whose son's acquaintance has made many hours happy in the life of Elia, used to allow a pound of Epping to every hare. Perhaps that was over-doing it. But, in spite of the note of Philomel, who, like some fine poets, that think no scorn to adopt plagiarisms from an humble brother, reiterates every Spring her cuckoo cry of 'Jug, Jug, Jug,' Elia pronounces that a hare, to be truly palated, must be roasted. Jugging sophisticates her. In *our* way it eats so 'crips,' as Mrs. Minikin says. Time was, when Elia was not arrived at his taste, that he preferred to all luxuries a roasted Pig. But he disclaims all such green-sickness appetites in future, though he hath to acknowledge the receipt of many a delicacy in that kind from correspondents – good, but mistaken men – in consequence of their erroneous supposition, that he had carried up into mature life the prepossessions of childhood. From the worthy Vicar of Enfield he acknowledges a tithe contribution of extraordinary sapor. The ancients must have loved hares. Else why adopt the word *lepores* (obviously from *lepus*) but for some subtle analogy between the delicate flavour of the latter, and the finer relishes of wit in what we most poorly translate *pleasantries*. The fine madnesses of the poet are the very decoction of his diet. Thence is he hare-brained. Harum-scarum is a libellous unfounded phrase of modern usage. 'Tis true the hare is the most circumspect of animals, sleeping with her eye open. Her ears, ever erect, keep them in that wholesome exercise, which conduces them to form the very tit-bit of the admirers of this noble animal. Noble will I call her, in spite of her detractors, who from occasional demonstrations of the principle of self-preservation (common to all animals) infer in her a defect of heroism. Half a hundred horsemen with thrice the number of dogs, scour the country in pursuit of puss across three counties; and because the well-flavoured beast, weighing the odds, is willing to evade the hue and cry, with her delicate ears shrinking perchance from discord – comes the grave Naturalist, Linnæus perchance or Buffon, and gravely sets down the Hare as a – timid animal. Why, Achilles, or Bully Dawson, would have declined the preposterous combat.

In fact, how light of digestion we feel after a hare! How tender its processes after swallowing! What chyle it promotes! How etherial! as if its living celerity were a type of its nimble coursing through the animal juices. The notice might be longer. It is intended less as a Natural History of the Hare, than a cursory thanks to the country 'good Unknown.' The hare has many friends, but none sincerer than

ELIA.

The Last Peach

I am the miserablest man living. Give me counsel, dear Editor. I was bred up in the strictest principles of honesty, and have passed my life in punctual adherence to them. Integrity might be said to be ingrained in our family. Yet I live in constant fear of one day coming to the gallows.

Till the latter end of last Autumn I never experienced these feelings of self-mistrust, which ever since have embittered my existence. From the apprehension of that unfortunate man whose story began to make so great an impression upon the public about that time, I date my horrors. I never can get it out of my head that I shall some time or other commit a forgery, or do some equally vile thing. To make matters worse I am in a banking-house. I sit surrounded with a cluster of bank-notes. These were formerly no more to me than meat to a butcher's dog. They are now as toads and aspics. I feel all day like one situated amidst gins and pitfalls. Sovereigns, which I once took such pleasure in counting out, and scraping up with my little tin shovel (at which I was the most expert in the banking-house), now scald my hands. When I go to sign my name I set down that of another person, or write my own in a counterfeit character. I am beset with temptations without motive. I want no more wealth than I possess. A more contented being than myself, as to money matters, exists not. What should I fear?

When a child I was once let loose, by favour of a nobleman's gardener, into his Lordship's magnificent fruit garden, with full leave to pull the currants and the gooseberries; only I was interdicted from touching the wall fruit. Indeed, at that season (it was the end of Autumn) there was little left. Only on the South wall (can I forget the hot feel of the brick-work?) lingered the one last peach. Now peaches are a fruit which I always had, and still have, an almost utter aversion to. There is something to my palate singularly harsh and repulsive in the flavour of them. I know not by what demon of contradiction inspired, but I was haunted with an irresistible desire to pluck it. Tear myself as often as I would from the spot, I found myself still recurring to it, till, maddening with desire, (desire I cannot call it,) with wilfulness rather – without appetite – against appetite, I may call it – in an evil hour I reached out my hand, and plucked it. Some few raindrops just then fell; the sky (from a bright day) became overcast; and I was a type of our first parents, after the eating of that fatal fruit. I felt myself naked and ashamed; stripped of my virtue, spiritless. The downy fruit, whose sight rather than savour had tempted me, dropped from my hand, never to be tasted. All the commentators in the world cannot persuade me but that the Hebrew word in the second chapter of Genesis, translated apple, should be rendered peach. Only this way can I reconcile that mysterious story.

Just such a child at thirty am I among the cash and

valuables, longing to pluck, without an idea of enjoyment further. I cannot reason myself out of these fears: I dare not laugh at them. I was tenderly and lovingly brought up. What then? Who that in life's entrance has seen the babe F—, from the lap stretching out his little fond mouth to catch the maternal kiss, could have predicted, or as much as imagined, that life's very different exit? The sight of my own fingers torments me; they seem so admirably constructed for – pilfering. Then the jugular vein which I have in common —; in an emphatic sense may I say with David, I am 'fearfully made.' All my mirth is poisoned by these unhappy suggestions. If, to dissipate reflection, I hum a tune, it changes to the 'Lamentations of a Sinner.' My very dreams are tainted. I awake with a shocking feeling of my hand in some pocket.

Advise me, dear Editor, on this painful heart-malady. Tell me, do you feel any thing allied to it in yourself? Do you never feel an itching, as it were – a *dactylomania* – or am I alone? You have my honest confession. My next may appear from Bow-street.

SUSPENSURUS.

A Few Words on Christmas

Close the shutters, and draw the curtains together, and pile fresh wood upon the hearth! Let us have, for once, an innocent *auto da fè*. Let the hoarded corks be brought forth, and branches of crackling laurel. Place the wine and fruit and the hot chestnuts upon the table. And now, good folks and children, bring your chairs round to the blazing fire. Put some of those rosy apples upon your plates. We'll drink one glass of bright sherry 'to our absent friends and readers,' and then let us talk a little about Christmas.

And what is Christmas?

Why, it is the happiest time of the year. It is the season of mirth and cold weather. It is the time when Christmas-boxes and jokes are given; when mistletoe, and red-berried laurel, and soups, and sliding, and school-boys, prevail; when the country is illuminated by fires and bright faces; and the town is radiant with laughing children. Oranges, as rich as the fruit of the Hesperides, shine out in huge golden heaps. Cakes, frosted over (as if to rival the glittering snow) come forth by thousands from their summer (caves) ovens: and on every stall at every corner of every street are the roasted apples, like incense fuming on Pagan altars.

And *this* night is CHRISTMAS EVE. Formerly it was a serious and holy vigil. Our forefathers observed it strictly till a certain hour, and then requited their own forbearance with cups of ale and Christmas candles, with placing the *yule clog* on the fire, and roaring themselves thirsty till morning. Time has altered this. We are neither so good as our forefathers were – nor so bad. We go to bed sober; but we have forgotten their old devotions. Our conduct looks like a sort of compromise; so that we are not worse than our ancestors, we are satisfied not to be better: but let that pass. What we now call Christmas Eve – (there is something very delightful in old terms: they had always their birth in reason or sentiment) was formerly *Mædrenack*, or *The Night of Mothers*! How beautifully does this recall to one's heart that holy tale – that wonderful nativity, which the Eastern shepherds went by night to gaze at and adore –

> (It was the winter wild,
> When the heaven-born child
> All meanly wrapp'd in the rude manger lay;)

a prodigy, which, had it been invention only, would have contained much that was immaculate and sublime; but, twined as it is with man's hopes and fears, is invested with a grand and overwhelming interest.

But to-night is Christmas Eve, and so we will be merry. Instead of toast and ale, we will content ourselves with our sherry and chestnuts; and we must put up with coffee or fragrant tea, instead of having the old *Wassail-bowl* which formed part of the inspiration of our elder poets. We were once admitted to the mysteries of that fine invention, and we respect it accordingly. Does anyone wish to know its merits? Let him try what he can produce, on our hint, and be grateful to us for ever. 'The Wassail-bowl' is, indeed, a great composition. It is not carved by Benvenuto Cellini (the outside *may*, – but it is not material), nor shaped by Michael Angelo from the marble quarries of Carrara; but it is a liquor fit for the lips of the Indian Bacchus, and worthy to celebrate his return from conquest. It is made – for, after all, we must descend to particulars – it is made of wine, with *some* water (but parce, precor, precor!) with spices of various sorts, and roasted apples, which float in triumph upon its top. The proportions of each are not important – in fact, they should be adapted to the taste of the drinkers. The only caution that seems necessary is to 'spare the water.' If the Compositor should live in the neighbourhood of Aldgate, this hint may be deemed advisable; though we mean no affront to either him or the pump.

One mark and sign of Christmas is the *music*; rude enough, indeed, but generally gay, and speaking eloquently of the season. Music, at festival times, is common to most countries. In Spain, the serenader twangs his guitar: in Italy, the musician allures rich notes from his Cremona: in Scotland, the bagpipe drones out its miserable noise: in Germany, there is the horn, and the pipe in Arcady. We too, in our turn, have our Christmas '*Waits*,' who witch us at early morning, before cock-crow, with strains and welcomings which belong to night. They wake us so gently that the music seems to have commenced in our dreams, and we listen to it till we sleep again. Besides this, we have our songs, from the young and the old, jocose and fit for the time. What old gentleman of sixty has not his stock – his one, or two, or three frolicksome verses. He sings them for the young folks, and is secure of their applause and his own private satisfaction. His wife, indeed, perhaps says '*Really*, my dear Mr. Williams, you should *now* give over these, etc.'; but he is more resolute from opposition, and gambols through his 'Flowery Meads of May,' or 'Beneath a shady bower,' while the children hang on his thin, trembling, untuneable notes in delighted and delightful amaze.

Many years ago (some forty-one, – or two, – or three) when we were at home 'for the Christmas holidays,' we occasionally heard these things. What a budget of songs we had! None of them were good for much; but they were sung by joyful spirits, amidst fun and laughter, loud and in defiance of tune, and we were enchanted. There was 'Bright Chanticleer proclaims the dawn,' – and ''Twas in the good ship Rover,' – and, 'Buy my matches,' – (oh! what an accompaniment there was with the flat hand and the elbow) – 'The lobster claw,' – and others. We should be sorry to strip them, like 'Majesty' in the riddle, of their merit first and last (our recollection) and reduce them to 'a jest.' Yet they were indeed a jest, and a very pleasant one. – Of all the songs, however, which become a time of feasting, there is none comparable to one written by Beaumont and Fletcher. It is racy, and rich, and sparkling. It has the strength and regal taste of Burgundy, and the ethereal spirit of champaigne. Does the reader wish to see it? Here it is: the words seem floating in wine.

GOD LYÆUS – ever young,
Ever honour'd, ever sung;
Stain'd with blood of lusty grapes,
In a thousand lusty shapes,

Dance upon the mazer's brim,
In the crimson liquor swim;
From thy plenteous hand divine
Let a river run with wine!

What a rioter was he that wrote this! His drink was not water from Hippocrene. His fountain flowed with wine. His goddess was a girl with purple lips; and his dreams were rich, like the autumn; but prodigal, wild, and Bacchanalian!

Leaving now our *eve* of Christmas, its jokes, and songs, and warm hearths, we will indulge ourselves in a few words upon CHRISTMAS DAY. It is like a day of victory. Every house and church is as green as spring. The laurel, that never dies, – the holly, with its armed leaves and scarlet berries, – the mistletoe, under which one sweet ceremonial is (we hope still) performed, are seen. Every brave shrub that has life and verdure seems to come forward to shame the reproaches of men, and to show them that the earth is never dead, never parsimonious. Then, what gay dresses are intermixed, – Art rivalling Nature! Woe to the rabbits and the hares, and the nut-cracking squirrels, the foxes, and all children of the woods, for furriers shall spoil them of their coats, to keep woman (the wonder of creation) warm! And woe to those damsels (fair anachronisms) who will not fence out the sharp winter; for rheumatisms and agues shall be theirs, and catarrhs shall be their portion in spring. But, look! what thing is this, awful and coloured like the rainbow, – blue, and red, and glistening yellow? Its vest is sky-tinctured! The edges of its garments are like the sun! Is it

— A faery vision
Of some gay creature of the element,
That in the colours of the rainbow lives,
And plays i' the plighted clouds?

No; – it is the Beadle of St. —'s! How Christmas and consolatory he looks! How redolent of good cheer is he! He is a cornu-copia, – an abundance! What pudding-sleeves! – what a collar, red and like a beef-steak, is his! He is a walking refreshment! He looks like a *whole* parish, – full, important, – but untaxed. The children of charity gaze at him with a modest smile, the straggling boys look on him with confidence. They do not pocket their marbles. They do not fly from the familiar gutter. This is a red-letter day; and the cane is reserved for to-morrow.

London is not *too* populous at Christmas. But what there is of population looks more alive than at other times. Quick walking and heaps of invitations keep the blood warm. Every one seems hurrying to a dinner. The breath curls upward like smoke through the frosty air; the eyes glisten; the teeth are shown; the muscles of the face are rigid, and the colour of the cheek has a fixed look, like a stain. Hunger is no longer an enemy. We feed him, like the ravenous tiger, till he pants and sleeps, or is quiet. Everybody eats at Christmas. The rich feast as usual; but the tradesman leaves his moderate fare for dainties. The apprentice abjures his chop, and plunges at once into the luxuries of joints and puddings. The schoolboy is no longer at school. He dreams no more of the coming lesson or the lifted rod; but mountains of jelly rise beside him, and blanc-mange, with its treacherous foundations, threatens to overwhelm his fancy; roods of mince pies spread out their chequered riches before him; and figures (only real on the 6th of January) pass by him, one by one, like ghosts before the vision of the King of Scotland. Even the servant has his 'once a year' bottle of port; and the beggar his 'alderman in chains.'

Oh! merry piping time of Christmas! Never let us permit thee to degenerate into distant courtesies and formal salutations. But let us shake our friends and familiars by the hand, as our fathers and their fathers did. Let them all come around us, and let us count how many the year has added to our circle. Let us enjoy the present, and laugh at the past. Let us tell old stories and invent new ones – innocent always, and ingenious if we can. Let us not meet to abuse the world, but to make it better by our individual example. Let us be patriots, but not men of party. Let us look *of the time*, – cheerful and generous, and endeavour to make others as generous and cheerful as ourselves.

GREAT FOOD

THROUGHOUT the history of civilization, food has been livelihood, status symbol, entertainment – and passion. The twenty fine food writers here, reflecting on different cuisines from across the centuries and around the globe, have influenced each other and continue to influence us today, opening the door to the wonders of every kitchen.

THE WELL-KEPT KITCHEN .... *Gervase Markham*
THE JOYS OF EXCESS .... *Samuel Pepys*
EVERLASTING SYLLABUB AND THE ART OF CARVING .... *Hannah Glasse*
RECIPES FROM THE WHITE HART INN .... *William Verrall*
A DISSERTATION UPON ROAST PIG & Other Essays .... *Charles Lamb*
THE PLEASURES OF THE TABLE .... *Brillat-Savarin*
THE ELEGANT ECONOMIST .... *Eliza Acton*
THE CHEF AT WAR .... *Alexis Soyer*
THE CAMPAIGN FOR DOMESTIC HAPPINESS .... *Isabella Beeton*
NOTES FROM MADRAS .... *Colonel Wyvern*
EXCITING FOOD FOR SOUTHERN TYPES .... *Pellegrino Artusi*
FROM ABSINTHE TO ZEST .... *Alexandre Dumas*
BUFFALO CAKE AND INDIAN PUDDING .... *Dr A. W. Chase*
A LITTLE DINNER BEFORE THE PLAY .... *Agnes Jekyll*
MURDER IN THE KITCHEN .... *Alice B. Toklas*
LOVE IN A DISH & Other Pieces .... *M. F. K. Fisher*
A TASTE OF THE SUN .... *Elizabeth David*
A MIDDLE EASTERN FEAST .... *Claudia Roden*
EATING WITH THE PILGRIMS & Other Pieces .... *Calvin Trillin*
RECIPES AND LESSONS FROM A DELICIOUS COOKING REVOLUTION .... *Alice Waters*